ELIZABETH McCRACKEN

Elizabeth McCracken is the author of *An Exact Replica of My Imagination*, *The Giant's House*, *Here's Your Hat What's Your Hurry*, and *Niagara Falls All Over Again*. A former public librarian, she is now a faculty member at the University of Texas, Austin. Her work has been shortlisted for the National Book Award and she was also chosen as one of *Granta*'s 20 Best American Writers Under 40.

ALSO BY ELIZABETH McCRACKEN

Here's Your Hat What's Your Hurry
The Giant's House
Niagara Falls All Over Again
An Exact Replica of a Figment of My Imagination: A Memoir

ELIZABETH McCRACKEN

Thunderstruck

& Other Stories

VINTAGE

2 4 6 8 10 9 7 5 3 1

Vintage
20 Vauxhall Bridge Road,
London SW1V 2SA

Vintage is part of the Penguin Random House group of companies
whose addresses can be found at global.penguinrandomhouse.com

Penguin
Random House
UK

Selected stories in this work were previously published in the
following: 'Something Amazing' in *Zoetrope: All-Story*; 'Property' in
Granta and subsequently in *The Best American Short Stories* (2011);
'Some Terpischore' in *Zoetrope: All-Story* and subsequently in
The Pushcart Prize 2006 and *The Ecco Anthology of Contemporary
American Short Fiction*; 'Juliet' in *Esquire*; 'Hungry' in *Ploughshares*;
'The Lost & Found Department of Greater Boston' in *Zoetrope:
All-Story*; 'Thunderstruck' in *Story Quarterly*.

First published in Great Britain in 2014 by
Jonathan Cape

www.vintage-books.co.uk

A CIP catalogue record for this book is available from the British Library

ISBN 9780099592976

Printed and bound by Clays Ltd, St Ives plc

For Edward
for every reason

CONTENTS

Thunderstruck

Something Amazing

Just west of Boston, just north of the turnpike, the ghost of Missy Goodby sleeps curled up against the cyclone fence at the dead end of Winter Terrace, dressed in a pair of ectoplasmic dungarees. That thumping noise is Missy bopping a plastic Halloween pumpkin on one knee; that flash of light in the corner of a dark porch is the moon off the glasses she wore to correct her lazy eye. Late at night when you walk your dog and feel suddenly cold, and then unsure of yourself, and then loathed by the world, that's Missy Goodby, too, hissing as she had when she was alive and six years old, *I hate you, you stink, you smell, you* baby.

The neighborhood kids remember Missy. She bit when she was angry and pinched no matter what. They don't feel sorry for her ghost self. They remember the funeral they were forced to attend after she died, how her mother threw herself on the coffin, wailing, how they thought she was kidding and so laughed out loud and got shushed. The way the neighborhood kids tell the story, the coffin was lowered into the ground and Missy Goodby's grieving mother leapt down and then had to be yanked from the hole like a weed. Everyone always believes the better story eventually. Really, Joyce Goodby just thumped the coffin at the graveside service. Spanked it: two little spanks, nothing serious. She knew that pleading would never budge her daughter, not because she was dead but because she was stubborn. All her life, the more you pleaded with Missy, the more likely she was to do something to terrify you. Joyce Goodby spanked the coffin and walked away and listened for footsteps behind her. She walked all the way home, where she took off her shoes, black pumps with worn stones of gray along the toes. "Done with *you,*" she told them.

The soul is liquid, and slow to evaporate. The body's a bucket and liable to slosh. Grieving, haunted, heartbroken, obsessed: your friends will tell you to *cheer up*. What they really mean is *dry up*. But it isn't a matter of will. Only time and light will do the job.

Who wants to, anyhow?

Best keep in the dark and nurse the damp. Cover the mirrors, keep the radio switched off. Avoid the newspaper, the television, the whole outdoors, anywhere little girls congregate, though the world is manufacturing them hand over fist, though there are now, it seems, more little girls living in the world than any other variety of human being. Or middle-aged men whose pants don't fit, or infant boys, or young women with wide, sympathetic, fretful foreheads. Whatever you have lost there are more of, just not yours. Sneeze. Itch. Gasp for breath. Seal the windows. Replace the sheets, then the mattresses. Pry the mercury from your teeth. Buy appliances to scrub the air.

Even so, the smell of the detergent from the sheets will fall into your nose. The chili your nice son cooks will visit you in the bedroom. The sweat from his clothes when he runs home from high school, the fog of his big yawping shoes, the awful smell of batteries loaded into a remote control, car exhaust, the plastic bristles on your tooth-brush, the salt-air smell of baking soda once you give up toothpaste. Make your house as safe and airtight as possible. Filter the air, boil the water: the rashes stay, the wheezing gets worse.

What you are allergic to can walk through walls.

The neighborhood kids don't remember what Joyce Goodby looked like back when she regularly drove down Winter Terrace; they've forgotten her curly black hair, her star-and-moon earrings, her velvet leggings. It's been five years. Now that she's locked away, they know everything about her. She no longer cuts or colors her mercury hair but instead twists it like a towel and pins it to her head. The paper face mask she wears over her nose and mouth makes her eyes look big. Her clothes are unbleached cotton and hemp; an invalid could eat them. She and her son, Gerry, used to look alike, a pair of freckled hearty people. Not anymore. Her freckles have starved from lack of light. Her eyebrows are thick, her eyelashes thin. She seems made of soap and steel wool.

Something's wrong in the neighborhood, she tells her son, it gave Missy lymphoma and now it's made her sick.

Of course she's a witch. The older kids tell younger kids, and kids who live on the street tell the kids round the corner. The Winter Terrace Witch, they call her, as though she's a seventeenth-century legend. She eats children. She kills them. She killed her own daughter a million years ago.

Some gangly kid not even from the street tells Santos and Johnny Mackers about the witch and the ghost. The Mackerses have just moved to Winter Terrace. Santos is nine years old, with curly hair and a strange accent, the result of nearly a decade of post-nasal drip. Johnny is as tough a five-year-old as ever was, a preschool monster Santos has created on the sly. Santos steals their father's Kools and lights them for Johnny. He has taught Johnny all the swears he knows, taught him how to punch, all in hopes that their mother will love Johnny a little less and him a little more. It's not working. Already they're famous on the street, where no one has ever seen Johnny Mackers's feet touch the ground. He rides his Big Wheel everywhere: up and down the street and into the attached garage. He rides it directly into the cyclone fence.

"You're a crazy motherfucker," Santos says. "A crazy motherfucker." He doesn't like the word himself but Johnny won't learn it otherwise.

"That's Ghostland, by the fence," the gangly kid says, from the other side. "That's where all the ghosts get caught, that's why they call it a dead end."

"Nosir," says Santos.

"Yessir," says the kid. "Dead girl ghost. Plus there's a witch." He spits to be tough but he hasn't practiced enough: he just drools, then walks away, embarrassed.

Johnny Mackers is swarthy and black-haired and Italian-looking, like his mother; Santos has his Irish father's looks. He likes to shut Johnny into things. Already he's investigated the locks of their new house. The attic, the basement, the mirror-fronted closet in their parents' room: every lock sounds different, key, slide bolt, knob, hook-and-eye, dead bolt. He's glad to learn of a ghost to threaten Johnny with. "The dead girl wants to kiss you. Here she comes. Pucker up." But the dead girl isn't interested, and Johnny Mackers knows it. The neighborhood kids are lying when they say they see her. The dead girl doesn't watch as Santos stuffs Johnny into the front hall closet. The dead girl doesn't see the fingers at the bottom of the door, or the foot that stomps on them. She doesn't see Mrs. Mackers open up the door an hour later, saying, "What are you doing in there, for Pete's sake? The way you hide, it drives me nuts. Why don't you go ride your bike. Go on, now." The dead girl doesn't sleep outside, ever. Why would she? She is with her mother, who—as she cleans the kitchen (her eyesight so vigilant she can see individual motes of dust, a single bacterium scuttling along the countertop)—can hear the mortar-and-pestle sound of a plastic wheel grinding along the grit of the gutter, a noise that should surely mean more than a grimy black-haired boy getting from one end of the street to another.

. . .

A different child might have turned into a different kind of ghost, visible only to little children, a finder of lost balls, a demander of candy. She could have visited Johnny Mackers late at night, when he plotted how he would kill his brother Santos. She could have haunted Santos himself. She could have accomplished things.

Instead, she likes to snuffle close to her mother's skin. The best spot is Joyce's skin in the hollow just below her cheekbones and just above her jaw: you have to get close, you have to get nearly under Joyce's nose to settle in. Sometimes Missy gets in the way and cuts off her mother's breath. She doesn't mean to. The biting, pinching child bites and pinches, along her mother's arms, her pale stomach.

"Look," Joyce says to her son, and displays her forearms, which are captioned with strange anaglyphic sentences, spelled out in hives.

Gerry Goodby was twelve when his little sister died. Now he's a seventeen-year-old six-foot-tall lacrosse player. He has watched his mother turn from a human woman into some immaculate vegetable substance, wan, thin, lamplit. *What will you do,* his father says. He means about college. For the past five years, Gerry and his father have had the same alternating conversation. *I want to live with you,* Gerry will say, and his father will answer, *You know that's impossible, you know your mother needs you.* Or his father will say, *This is crazy, she's crazy, come live with me,* and Gerry will answer, *You know that's impossible.*

He was the one who closed up Missy's room. A year after she died, his mother wheezing, weeping, molting on the sofa. She gave him the directions. *Don't touch a thing.*

Just seal it up. He nailed over the doorway with barrier cloth, then painted over that with latex paint. His mother felt better for nearly a month.

Sometimes he stops in the hallway and touches the slumped wall where Missy's door used to be. He feels like a projection on a screen, waiting for the rest of the movie to be filled in. *This is intolerable,* he thinks. He's always thought of *intolerable* as a grown-up word, like *mortgage.*

Missy the allergen, Missy the poison. She's everywhere in the house, no matter how their mother scrubs and sweeps and burns and purges. She's in the bricks. She's in the new bedding, in the nontoxic cleaning fluid. She leeches and fumes and wishes—insofar as ghosts can, in the way that water wishes, and has a will, sometimes thwarted and sometimes not—that the house were not shut up so tight. She rises to the ceiling daily and collects there, drips down, tries again. Outside there's a world of blank skin, waiting for her to scribble all over it.

"I would die without you," Joyce Goodby tells her son one morning. He knows it's true, just as he knows he's the only one who would care. Sometimes he thinks it wouldn't be such a bad bargain, his mother's death for his own freedom. Anyone would understand. Anyhow, it's time to leave for school. She won't die during the school day; at least, she hasn't so far.

Across the street Santos shuts Johnny Mackers in a steamer trunk in the attic instead of walking him to kindergarten. Then Santos, liberated, guilty, decides to skip school himself. He walks to the corner and gets on the bus that says, across its forehead, *DOWNTOWN VIA PIKE.* He has just enough change to pay his fare. The bus is crammed with people. A man in a gray windbreaker stands up. "Hey," he says. "Kiddo. Sit here."

Santos sits.

The world goes on. The world will. At any moment you can look from your window and see your neighbors. The fat couple who live next door will bicker and then bear hug each other. The teenage boys will play basketball with their shirts off. The elderly lady next door waits for the visiting nurse; her bloodhound snoozes in the sun like a starlet, one paw across his snout. You want to drape that old, good, big dog's sun-warmed fawn-colored ears on your fists. You want to reassure the elderly lady, tease the fat couple, watch—just watch—those shirtless, heedless boys. *You have to get out,* your family says, *it's time. It's time to join the world again.* But you never left the world. You're filled with tenderness, with worry for every living being, but you can't do anything—not for your across-the-street neighbors, or for the people on the next street, or around the corner, or driving on the turnpike two blocks away, or in the city, or the whole country, the whole world, west and east and north and south. You are so unlucky you don't want to brush up against anyone who isn't.

You will not join a group. You will not read a book. You're not interested in anyone else's story, not when your own story takes up all your time. When the calamity happened, your friends said, *It's so sad. It's the worst kind of luck,* and you could tell they believed it. What's changed?

You are as sad and unlucky as you were when it happened. It's still so, so sad. It's still the worst kind of luck.

The dead live on in the homeliest of ways. They're listed in the phone book. They get mail. Their wigs rest on Styrofoam heads at the back of closets. Their beds are made. Their shoes are everywhere.

The paint across the door is still tacky. It's dumb to even be here. Joyce swears she can smell the fiberboard headboard of the bed through the barrier cloth, the scratch-and-sniff stickers on the desk, the old lip gloss, the bubble bath in containers shaped like animals arranged on the dresser top, the unchanged mattress, the dust. The dress from Bloomingdale's that had been hers and then Missy's, in striped fabric like a railroad engineer's hat. The Mexican jumping beans bought at a joke shop before the diagnosis, four dark little beans in a plastic box with a clear top and blue bottom that clasped shut like an old-fashioned change purse. You warmed them in your hands, and they woke up and twitched and flipped: the worms who lived inside dozed in the cold but threw themselves against the walls when the temperature rose.

"Worms?" Missy had asked. Her nose was lacy with freckles, pink around the rim. "How do we feed them?"

"We don't," said Joyce.

"Then they'll starve to death!"

Quickly Joyce made up a story: the worm wasn't a worm, it was a soul. It was fine where it was, it was eternal, and if the bean stopped moving that only meant the soul had moved on to find another home. *Back to Mexico?* asked Missy, and Joyce said, *Sure, why not.* (Who knows? Maybe that's why the worms woke up when they got warm—they thought, *At last we're back home in Oaxaca.*) Back then, reincarnation was a comforting fable. In fairy tales, people were always born again as beasts, frogs, migrating swans.

Now Joyce feels the world shake and thinks, *Mexican jumping bean.* She can't decide whether the house is the bean and she's the worm, or the bean's her body and the worm her soul.

Neither: someone has wrenched open the wooden storm door of the sun porch and let it slam behind him. Then the doorbell rings.

Johnny Mackers has escaped. He's kicked his way out of the trunk, the one his great-grandmother emigrated from Ireland with, still lined with the napkins and tablecloths she thought she'd need for a new life. She once told Johnny a story about a monkey that belonged to a rich family she worked for, and though he knows that monkey died in the rich family's house, he was sure the trunk smelled of monkey, as well as the inventory of every story his great-grandmother ever told him: whiskey, lamp oil, house fires, a scalded baby's arm treated with butter, horse sweat, lemon drops, the underside of wooden dentures. The trunk turned out to be made of cardboard held together with moldy oak and cheap tin. He kicked one end to pieces and crawled out. The wreckage scared him. It was as though he'd kicked his great-grandmother apart before she'd had a chance to get on the boat and sail to Boston and meet her future husband at an amusement park and have children.

He rings the doorbell once, twice. Last year in their old neighborhood he helped Santos sell mints for the Y; you were supposed to ring, count to ten slowly, and ring only once more. He counts to ten but quickly and over and over. To keep himself from ringing too many times, he runs a finger over the engraved sign by the bell. He doesn't know what a solicitor is or that he's one. The air of the sun porch is stale. He gulps at it. The front door opens.

"Lady," he says, "do you wanna buy a rock?"

The rocks in Johnny Mackers's hand have been lightly rubbed with crayon. He found them a week ago at Revere Beach with his father: at the beach they were washed by the water and looked valuable and ancient. Dry, they turned gray and merely old. The woman who has answered the door is the witch, of course, the dead girl's mother. He's come to her first of all the neighbors because she may be able to grant wishes, and Johnny has one. When it's the right time, he'll ask: he wishes his brother dead. She's the cleanest person he's ever seen and yet not entirely white. Everything about her is blurred, like dirt beneath the surface of a hockey rink.

He would do anything for her. He knows that right away, too. You have to, to get your wish granted.

He has cobwebs in his hair but she doesn't smell them. She doesn't smell the cigarette smoke or the fibers off the wall-to-wall carpet or the must that clings to him from the trunk, the usual immigrant disappointments, the rusty cut on his ankle that needs medical attention. What she smells is little-kid sweat touched with sweet bland tomato sauce. Ketchup, canned spaghetti, maybe.

"Come in," she says. "I'll find my purse."

Once he's inside she doesn't know what to do. She sits him at the kitchen table and offers him a plate of pebbly brown cookies. He eats one. He would rather something chocolate and store-bought, but his mother likes cookies like this, studded with sesame seeds, and he knows that eating them is a good deed. She hooks a cobweb out of his hair with one finger. He picks up another cookie and rubs the side of his cheek with the back of one wrist.

"You need a bath," she says.

"OK," he answers.

Now, Joyce. You can't just bathe someone else's child. You can't invite a strange boy into your house and bring him upstairs and say, "Chop chop. Off with your clothes. Into your bath."

The bathroom is yellow and pink. Johnny Mackers understands his new obedience as a kind of sanitary bewitching. He is never naked in front of his mother like this: his mother likes to pinch. "Just a little!" she'll say, and she'll pinch him on his knee and stomach and everywhere. Santos is right, their mother loves Johnny best. His hatred of kisses and hugs has turned her into a pinching tickler, a sneak thief. "Just a little little!" she'll say, when she sees any pinchable part of him.

"Bubbles?" Joyce asks, and he nods. But there's no bubble bath. Instead she pours the entire bottle of shampoo into the tub.

So it's true, what the neighborhood kids say. She does kidnap children.

He's not circumcised. He looks like an Italian sculpture from a dream, a polychrome putto from the corner of a church. The tub is rotten, pink, with a sliding glass door that looks composed of a million thumbprints. Soon the bubbles rise up like shrugging, foamy shoulders, cleft where the water from the faucet pours in.

The almond soap is as cracked as an old tooth. The boy steps over the tub edge. "Careful," Joyce says, as he puts his hand on the shower door runners. When Missy was born, Joyce was relieved: she loved her husband and son but there was, she thought, something different about a girl. Maybe it was scientific, those as-yet unused girl organs speaking to their authorial organs, transmitting information as though by radio. A strange little boy is easier to love than a strange little girl. The water slicking down his dirty hair reveals the angle and size of his ears. She soaps them and thinks of Missy in the tub, the fine long hair knotted at the nape, the big ears, the crescent shape where they attached to her head. The arch at the base of her skull.

"Your ears are very small," she says.

"I know," he answers.

She soaps the shoulder blades that slide beneath the boy's dark skin and is amazed to see that he's basically intact, well-fed, maybe even well-loved.

(Of course he is. Even now his mother is calling his name on the next block. Soon she'll phone the police.)

"What's your name?" Joyce asks.

He says, "I don't know."

"You don't know your name?"

He shrugs. He looks at his foam-filled hands. Then he says, "Johnny."

"What's your last name?"

"Lion," he says. He drops his face in the bubbly bath water, plunges his head down, and blubs.

When he comes up she says, smiling, "Your clothes are filthy. You're going to need clean ones. Where were you?"

"Trunk."

"Of a *car*?"

"Trunk like a suitcase," he answers. He pounds the sliding glass shower door, bored with questioning.

It's after school. Mrs. Mackers, the owlish pincher, is back on Winter Terrace, asking the neighborhood kids if they've seen Johnny, the little boy, the little boy on the trike. She doesn't know where Santos is, either, but Santos is old enough to take care of himself (though she's wrong in thinking this—Santos even now is in terrible trouble, Santos, miles away, is calling for her). The last teenage boy she asks is so freckled she feels sorry for him, a pause in her panic.

No, Gerry Goodby hasn't seen a little kid.

He's looking up at Missy's window; he always looks at it when he comes home, shouldering his lacrosse stick like a rifle. He didn't remember to pull down the blinds all the way before closing the room up and it always bothers him. You can see the edge of the dresser that overlaps the window frame, a darkened rainbow sticker, and just the snout-end of an enormous rocking horse named Blaze who used to say six different sentences when you pulled a cord in his neck. Blaze had been Gerry's horse first. It seemed unfair he had to disappear like that. Someday, Gerry knows, they'll have to sell the house, and the new owners will find the tomb of a six-year-old girl pharaoh. It's as though they've walled in Missy instead of burying her in the cemetery, as though (as in a ghost story) he will someday see her face looking back out at him, mouthing, *Why?* Gerry, in his head, always answers, *It's not your fault, you didn't know how dangerous you were.*

But this time he sees something appearing, then disappearing, then appearing again: the rocking horse showing its profile, one dark carved eye over and over.

Not only that: the front door is open.

The barrier cloth has been slit from top to bottom. Beyond it is the old door with the brassy doorknob still bright from all its years in the dark. Beyond the door is Missy's room.

"Hello," says his mother. She's sitting on the bed, smoothing a pair of light yellow overalls on her lap. There's a whole outfit set out next to her: the Lollipop brand underpants Missy had once written a song about, a navy turtleneck, an undershirt with a tiny rosebud at the sternum. The dust is everywhere in the room. It's a strange sort of dust, soot and old house, nothing human. Even so, compared to the rest of the house, this room is Oz. The comforter is pink gingham. The walls are pink with darker pink trim. Dolls of all nations lie along one wall, as though rubble from an earthquake has just been lifted from them. The

50-50 bedclothes are abrasive just to look at. He inhales. Nothing of Missy's fruit-flavored scent is left.

But his mother doesn't seem to notice. She has—he's heard this expression but never seen it—roses in her cheeks. "Look," she says, and points.

A boy. He's fallen through the chimney or he's a forgotten toy of Missy's come to life. What else can explain him here, brown and naked next to the rocking horse he's just dismounted, a gray towel turbaned around his head. He's pulling two-handed at the cord that works Blaze's voice box, but Blaze has had a stroke and can't speak, he just groans apologetically before the boy interrupts him with another tug. Through the half-drawn shades the police lights color Winter Terrace: blue, less blue, blue again.

Outside, the neighborhood kids sit on the sidewalk, their feet in the gutter, daring the cops to tell them to move along. The little smoking kid, the one who likes to swear, is missing. The kids are working on their story. *When did you last see him?* a policeman asks, but the fact is the woman, who is not crying yet, will get her boy back. That is, she'll get one of her boys back: the one she hasn't missed yet is missing for good, forever, and by tomorrow morning he will be his mother's favorite, and by tomorrow afternoon the police will have questioned everyone on the street, and the neighborhood kids will pretend that they remember Santos, though they can't even make sense of his name. He will pass into legend, too.

Inside Missy Goodby's room, Gerry obeys his mother: he looks at the little boy. He wonders how to sneak him back home. He wonders how to keep him forever.

Property

The ad should have read: *For rent, six-room hovel. Filled Mrs. Butterworth's bottle in living room, sandy sheets throughout, lingering smell.*

Or: *Wanted: gullible tenant for small house, must possess appreciation for chipped pottery, mid-1960s abstract silk-screened canvases, mouse-nibbled books on Georgia O'Keeffe.*

Or: *Available June: shithole.*

Instead, the posting on the college website called the house at 55 Bayberry Street old and characterful and sunny, furnished, charming, on a quiet street not far from the college and not far from the ocean. Large porch; separate artist's studio. Just right for the young married couple, then: Stony Badower and Pamela Graff, he thirty-nine, red-headed, pot-bellied, long-limbed, and beaky, a rare and possibly extinct bird; she blond and soft and hotheaded and German and sentimental. She looked like the plump-cheeked naughty heroine of a German children's book who'd just sawed off her own braids with a knife, looking for the next knifeable place. Her expression dared you to teach her a lesson. Like many sentimentalists, she was estranged from her family. Stony had never met them.

"America," she said that month. "All right. Your turn. Show me America." For the three years of their courtship and marriage they'd moved every few months. Berlin, Paris, Galway, near Odense, near Edinburgh, Rome, and now a converted stone barn in Normandy that on cold days smelled of cow pies and on hot days like the lost crayons of tourist children. Soon enough it would be summer, and the barn would be colossally expensive and filled with English people. Now it was time for Maine, where Stony had accepted a two-year job, cataloging a collection of 1960s underground publications: things printed on rice paper and Popsicle sticks and cocktail napkins. It fell to him to find the next place to live.

"We'll unpack my storage space," he said. "I have things."

"Yes, my love," she said. "I have things, too."

"You have a duffel bag. You have clothing. You have a saltshaker shaped like a duck, with a chipped beak."

She cackled a very European cackle, pride and delight in her ownership of the lusterware duck, whose name was Trudy. "The sole exhibit in the museum. When I am dead, people will know nothing about me." This was a professional opinion: she was a museum consultant. In Normandy she was helping set up an exhibition in a stone cottage that had been owned by a Jewish family deported during the war. In Paris, it had been the atelier of a minor artist who'd been the longtime lover of a major poetess; in Denmark, a workhouse museum. Her specialty was the air of recent evacuation: you knew something terrible had happened to the occupants but you hoped it might still be undone. She set historic spectacles on desktops and snuggled appropriate shoes under beds and did not overdust. Too much cleanliness made a place dead. In Rome she arranged an exhibit of the commonplace belongings of Ezra Pound: chewed pencils, drinking glasses, celluloid dice, dog-eared books. Only the brochure suggested a connection to greatness. At the Hans Christian Andersen Museum in Odense, where they were mere tourists, she lingered with admiration over Andersen's upper plate and the length of rope that he traveled with in case of hotel fire. "You can tell more from dentures than from years of diaries," she'd said then. "Dentures do not lie." She herself threw everything out. She did not want anyone to exhibit the smallest bit of her.

Now Stony said, solemnly, "I never want to drink out of Ikea glasses again. Or sleep on Ikea sheets. Or—and this one is serious—cook with Ikea pans. Your husband owns really expensive pans. How about that?"

"I am impressed, and you are bourgeois."

"Year lease," he said.

"I am terrified," said Pamela, smiling with her beautiful, angular un-American teeth, and then, "Perhaps we will afford to have a baby."

She was still, as he would think of it later, casually alive. In two months she would be, according to the doctors, *mi-*

raculously alive, and, later still, alive in a nearly unmodifiable twilight state. Or too modifiable: *technically* alive. Now she walked around the barn in her bra, which was as usual a little too small, and her underpants, as usual a little too big, though she was small-breasted and big-bottomed. Her red-framed glasses sat on her face at a tilt. "My ears are not plumb," she always said. It was one of the reasons they belonged together: they were flea-market people, put together out of odd parts. She limped. Even her name was pronounced with a limp, the accent on the second syllable. For a full month after they'd met he'd thought her name was Camilla, and he never managed to say it aloud without lining it up in his head beforehand—paMILLa, paMILLa— the way he had to collect German words for sentences ahead of time and then properly distribute the verbs. In fact he did that with English sentences, too, when speaking to Pamela, when she was alive.

He e-mailed the woman who'd listed the house—she was not the owner, she was working for the owners—and after a month of wrangling (she never sent the promised pictures; he was third in line, after a gaggle of students and a clutch of summer people; if the owners rented it out for the summer they could make a lot more money) managed to talk her into a yearlong lease, starting June 1.

The limp, it turned out, was the legacy of a stroke Pamela'd had in her early twenties that she'd never told him about. She had another one in the farmhouse two weeks before they were supposed to move; she hit her head on the metal Ikea counter as she fell. Stony's French was good enough only to ask the doctors how bad things were, but not to understand the answer. Pamela spoke the foreign languages; he cooked dinner; she proclaimed it delicious. In the hospital her tongue was unemployed, fat in her mouth, and she was fed through a tube. Someone had put her glasses on her face so that she would look more herself. A nurse came in hourly to straighten them. They did this as though her glasses were the masterpiece and all of Pamela the gallery wall—palms flat and gentle, leery of gravity. He sat in a molded green chair and dozed. One night he woke to the final nurse, who was straightening the glasses, and then the bedsheets. She turned to Stony. The last little bit of French he possessed drained out through the basin of his stomach.

"No?" he said.

This nurse was a small brown rabbit. Even her lips were brown. She wobbled on her feet as though deciding whether it was better if the mad husband caught and ate her now, or there should be a chase. Then she shrugged.

When someone dies it is intolerable to be shrugged at. He went back to the farmhouse to pack. First his suitcase, an enormous green nylon item with fretful, overworked zippers. Then Pamela's, that beige strap-covered duffel bag that looked like a midcentury truss. He had to leave France as soon as possible. He stuffed the bag with the undersized bras and oversized underpants, her favorite pair of creased black patent-leather loafers, an assortment of embroidered handkerchiefs. He, he needed a suitcase and a computer bag and then any number of plastic sacks to move from place to place, he collected souvenirs like vaccinations, but all of Pamela's belongings fit in the duffel. When he failed to find the duck, he remembered the words of the lovely Buddhist landlady in Edinburgh, when he'd apologized for breaking a large Italian bowl painted with plums: "We have a saying: it was already broken." Even now he wasn't sure if *we* meant Buddhists or Scots. He would leave a note for the landlady concerning the duck, but of course the loss of the duck could not destroy him.

The weight of Pamela's bag was like the stones in a suicide's pocket. Stony e-mailed his future boss, the kindly archivist, asked if he could straighten things out with the house—he would come, he would definitely come, but in the fall. *My wife has died,* he wrote, in rotten intelligible English. He'd wept already, and for hours, but suddenly he understood that the real thing was coming for him soon, a period of time free of wry laughter or distraction. The duffel bag he put in the closet for the French landlady to deal with. The ashes from the mortuary came in an urn, complete with a certificate that explained what they were, to show to customs officials. These he took with him to England, where he went for the summer to drink.

The Not-Owner of the house was a short, slightly creased, ponytailed blond woman in a baseball cap and a gleaming, fricative black tracksuit that suggested somewhere a husband dressed in the exact same outfit. She waved at him from the not particularly large front porch. For the past month she'd sent him cheerful e-mails about getting the lovely house ready for him, moving furniture, outfitting the kitchen, all of which came down to this: what have you spent your money on during your time on earth?

Books, art, cooking equipment. Oh, and a collection of eccentric but unuseful tables. That was it. Could they make room for tables, books, pots, pans, paintings? Of course, she wrote back. He'd chosen this house because it was not a sabbatical rental: even before—a word he now pronounced as a spondee, like B.C.—he longed to be reunited with his books, art, dishes, the doctor's table, the diner table, the various card catalogs, the side table made from an old cheese crate. He didn't want to live inside someone else's life, and sabbatical houses were always like that. You felt like a teenager who'd been given too much responsibility. Your parents were there frowning at you in the very arrangement of the furniture, how the spatulas were stored.

The house wasn't a Victorian, as he'd for some reason assumed, but an ordinary wood-framed house painted toothpaste blue. Amazing, how death made petty disappointments into operatic insults.

"Hello!" The woman whooshed across towards him. "I'm Carly. You're here. At last! It seems like ages ago we started talking about you and this house!"

The porch was psoriatic and decorated with a series of camp chairs. "I'm glad you found summer people," said Stony.

Carly nodded. "Yes. The last guy moved out this morning."

"Ah," said Stony, though they'd discussed this via e-mail over the last week. It was his ingratiating way, as a lifelong renter, to suggest unnecessary, helpful things, and he'd said he'd arrive on the fourth instead of the third so she'd have more time to arrange for cleaners.

"Here's the living room," she said. He followed her. Small, silky Carly, her head covered by the boy's cap. He felt like an about-to-be-retired greyhound being led by a jockey: big-nosed, cow-eyed, trying to be good despite his nerves. He might end up on a farm or destroyed, depending on which turn she took.

Not a jockey, of course, jockeys didn't ride greyhounds.

"Fireplace," said Carly. "Cable's still hooked up. Maybe you'll be lucky and they won't notice." A round-jawed teenager sat on a leather settee with a handheld video game, frowning at the screen like a Roman emperor impatient with the finickiness of his lions. "It's a nice room. These old houses have such character. This one—do you believe it?— it's a Sears, Roebuck kit. You picked it out of the catalog and it was delivered and assembled."

He could hear Pamela's voice: *This is not an old house.* The barn in Normandy was eighteenth century, the apartment in Rome even older. The walls were lined with homemade bookshelves, filled with paperback books: Ionesco, the full complement of Roths—Henry, Philip, Joseph. "Fireplace work?"

"There was a squirrel incident," said Carly vaguely. She swished across the entryway. "Dining room. The lease, I'm sure you'll remember, asks you to keep the corner cupboard locked." The cupboard in question looked filled with eye cups and egg cups and mustache cups. In the corner, a broken Styrofoam cooler had been neatly aligned beneath a three-legged chair; a white melamine desk had papers stuck in its jaw. *Kmart furniture,* he thought. Well, he'd have the movers take it down to the basement. "Kitchen's this way." The kitchen reminded him of his 1970s childhood and the awful taste of tongue depressors at the back of the throat. It looked as though someone had taken a potting shed and turned it inside out. A pattern of faux shingles crowned the honey-colored cupboards; the countertop Formica was patterned like a hospital gown. A round fluorescent light fixture cupped and backlit a collection of dead bugs. High above everything, a terra-cotta sun smiled down from the shingles with no sense of irony, or shame, whatsoever.

The smell of Febreze came down the stairs, wound around the smell of old cigarettes and something chemical, and worse. "Four bedrooms," said Carly. She led him up the stairs into one of the front rooms, furnished with a double mattress on a brown wooden platform. It looked like the sort of thing you'd store a kidnapped teenage girl underneath. The café curtains on the windows were badly water-stained and lightly cigarette-burned. "Listen!" said Carly. "It's a busy street, but you can't even hear it! Bedclothes in the closets. I need to get going," she said. "Tae kwon do. Settle in and let me know if there's anything else I can do for you, all right?"

He had not stood so close to a woman all summer, at least not while sober. He wanted to finger her ponytail, and then yank on it like a schoolyard bully. "Can I see the artist's studio?" he asked.

"Forgot!" she said. "Come along."

They walked through the scrubby backyard to a half-converted garage. "Lock sticks," said Carly, jiggling a door with a rice paper cataract over its window. "Looks dark in here till you turn on the lights."

The art studio was to have been Pamela's: she was a sometime jeweler and painter. Stony did not know whether it made things better or worse, that this space was the most depressing room he'd ever seen. The old blinds seemed stitched together of moth wings. A newsprint Picasso danced on a bulletin board. The smell of mildew was nearly physically painful. Along one wall a busted hollow-core door rested on sawhorses, and across the top, a series of shapes, huddled together as though for warmth. Pots, vases, bowls, all clearly part of the same family, the bluish gray of expensive cats. He expected them to turn and blink at him.

"My father was a potter," said Carly.

It took him a moment. "Ah! Your parents own this place?"

"My mom," said Carly. "She's an ob/gyn. Retired. You can't go anywhere in this town without meeting kids my mother delivered. She's like an institution. She's in New York now. There's a wheel, if you're interested. Think it still works. Potter's."

"No, thank you."

She sighed and snapped off the light.

They went back to the house. "All right, Pumpkin," she said, and the teenager stood up and revealed herself to be a girl, not a boy, with a few sharp, painful-looking pimples high on her cheeks and a long nose, and a smile that suggested that not everything was right with her. She shambled over to her little mother, and the two of them stood with their arms around each other.

Was she awkward, just? Brain-damaged? Carly reached up and curled a piece of hair behind her daughter's ear. It was possible, thought Stony, that all American teenagers might appear damaged to him these days, the way that all signs in front of fast-food restaurants—MAPLE CHEDDAR COMING SOON! MCRIB IS BACK—struck him as mysterious and threatening. "You OK?" Carly asked. The girl nodded and cuddled closer. The air in the Sears, Roebuck house— yes, he remembered now, that was something he would normally be intrigued by, a house built from a kit—felt tender and sad. *My wife has died,* he thought. He wondered whether Carly might say something. Wasn't now the time? *By the way, I'm sorry. I'm so sorry, what happened to you.* He had that thought sometimes these days. It wasn't grief, which he could be subsumed in at any moment, which like water bent all straight lines and spun whatever navigational tools he owned into nonsense—but a rational, detached thought: *Wasn't that awful, what happened to me, one, two, three months ago. That was a terrible thing for a person to go through.*

Carly said, "Tae kwon do. Call if you need me."

An empty package of something called Teddy Grahams. A half-filled soda bottle. Q-tips strewn on the bathroom floor. Mrs. Butterworth's, sticky, debased, a crime victim. Cigarette butts in one window well. Three condom wrappers behind the platform bed. Rubber bands in every drawer and braceleting every doorknob—why were old rubber bands so upsetting? The walls upstairs bristled with pushpins and the ghosts of pushpins and the square-shouldered shadows of missing posters. Someone had emptied several boxes of mothballs into the bedclothes that were stacked in the cupboards, and had thrown dirty bedclothes on top, and the idea of sorting through clean and dirty made him want to weep. The bath mat looked made of various flavors of old chewing gum. Grubby pencils lolled on desktops and in coffee mugs and snuggled along the baseboards. The dining-room tablecloth had been painted with scrambled egg and then scorched. The honey-colored kitchen was honey-sticky. The walls upstairs were bare and filthy; the walls downstairs covered in old art. The bookshelves were full. On the edges in front of the books were coffee rings and—there was no other word for it—detritus: part of a broken key ring, more pencils, half packs of cards. He had relatives like this. When he was a kid he loved their houses because of how nothing ever changed, how it could be 1971 outside and 1936 inside, and then he got a little older and realized that it was the same Vicks VapoRub on the bedside table, noticed how once a greeting card was stuck in a dresser mirror it would never be moved, understood that the jars of pennies did not represent possibility, as he'd imagined, but only jars and only pennies.

The landlords had filled the house with all their worst belongings and said, *This will be fine for other people.* A huge snarled antique rocker sat under an Indian print; the TV cart was fake wood and missing a wheel. The art on the walls—posters, silkscreened canvases—had been faded by the sun, but that possibly was an improvement.

The kitchen was objectively awful. Old bottles of oil

with the merest skim at the bottom crowded the counters. Half-filled boxes of a particularly cheap brand of biscuit mix had been sealed shut with packing tape. The space beneath the sink was filled, back to front, with mostly empty plastic jugs for cleaning fluids. After he opened the kitchen garbage can and a cloud of flies flew out, he called Carly from his newly purchased cell phone. Her voice was cracked with disappointment.

"Well, I can come back and pick up the garbage—"

"The house," said Stony, "is dirty. It's dirty. You need to get cleaners."

"I don't think Mom will go for that. She paid someone to clean in May—"

Pamela would have said, *Walk out. Sue for the rent and the deposit.* That is, he guessed she would. Then he was furious that he was conjuring up her voice to address this issue.

"The point," he said, "is not that it was clean in May. It's not clean now. It's a dirty house, and we need to straighten this out."

"I have things I have to do," said Carly. "I'll come over later."

Then the movers arrived, two men who looked like middle-aged yoga instructors. The boss exuded a strange calm that seemed possibly like the veneer over great rage. He whistled at the state of the house, and Stony wanted to hug him.

"Don't lose your cool," said the mover. "Hire cleaners, take it out of the rent." They unloaded all of Stony's old things, the doctor's table, the diner table, boxes of books, boxes of dishes, all the things he needed for his new life as a bourgeois widower. He really lived here. He felt pinned down by the weight of his belongings, and then decided it was not a terrible feeling. From the depths of his e-mail program he dug up a message from Carly that cc'd Sally Lasker, to whom he'd written the rent check. If he sat on the radiator at the back of the room and leaned, he could catch just a scrap of a wireless connection, and so he sat, and leaned, and sent what seemed to him a firm but sympathetic e-mail to Sally Lasker, detailing everything but her unfortunate taste in art.

Sally wrote back.

We cleaned the house in May, top to bottom, she wrote. *It took me a long time to dust the books, I did it myself. I cleaned the coffee rings off the bookcase. We laundered all the bedclothes. I'm sorry that the house is not what you expected. I'm sorry that the summer people have caused so much damage, that can't have been pleasant for you. But it seems that you are asking a great deal for a nine-month rental. We lived modestly all our lives, I'm afraid, and perhaps this is not what you pictured from Europe. I do feel as though we have bent over backwards for you so far.*

He went over this in a confused rage. What difference did it make that the house was clean in May? That there had been coffee rings before where coffee rings were now? He'd turned forty over the summer and it reminded him of turning eighteen. *I am not a child!* he wanted to yell. *I do not sleep on homemade furniture! I do not hide filthy walls with posters and Indian hangings!*

What did she mean, *bent over backwards*?

He stalked into the sweet Maine town and had two beers in a sports bar, and then stalked back. All the while he wrote to Sally in his head, and told her he was glad she'd found summer renters who'd made up the rent and maybe she had not heard what exactly had delayed his arrival.

When he found the wireless again, there was a new e-mail.

Hire the cleaners. Take the total out of the rent. I am sorry, and I hope this is the end of the problems. If you want to store anything precious, put it in the studio, not the basement. The basement floods.

So he couldn't even send his righteous e-mail.

That night he boxed up Sally's kitchen and took it to the basement, pulled the art from the walls and put it in the dank studio. He couldn't decide on what was a more hostile act, packing the filthy bath mat or throwing it away. Packing it, he decided, and so he packed it. He tumbled the mothball-filled bedclothes into garbage bags. He moved out the platform bed and slept on the futon sofa and went the next day to the nearby mall to buy his very own bed. The following Monday the cleaners came, looking like a Girls in Prison movie (missing teeth, tattoos, denim shorts, cleavage) and declared without prodding that the house was disgusting, and he felt a surge of actual happiness: yes, disgusting, it was, anyone could see it. He was amazed at how hard they worked. They cleaned out every cupboard. They hauled all those bottles to the curb. He tipped them extravagantly. One of the house cleaners left her number on several pieces of paper around the house—PERSONAL HOUSECLEANING CALL JACKIE $75—and the owner of the cleaning service called the next day to say that she'd heard one of the girls was offering to clean privately, was that true, it wasn't allowed, and Stony accidentally said yes, and was devastated that the perfect transaction of cleaning had been sullied. Then he called back and said he'd misunderstood, she hadn't, everything had been by the book.

That night he wrote Sally an e-mail explaining where he'd put things: kitchen goods boxed in basement, linens and art in the studio.

He painted the upstairs walls and hung his own art. He boxed up some of the resident books. Slowly he moved half the furniture to the studio and replaced it with things bought at auction. The kindly archivist, his boss, came by the house. "My God!" he said. "This place! You've made it look great. You know, I tried to get you out of the lease last May, but Sally wouldn't go for it. I tried to find you someplace nicer. But you've made it nice. Good for you."

At work he cataloged the underground collection, those beautiful daft objects of passion, pamphlets and buttons, broadsides. What would the founders of these publications make of him? What pleasure, to describe things that had been invented to defy description—but maybe he shouldn't have. The inventors never imagined these things lasting forever, filling phase boxes, the phase boxes filling shelves. He was a cartographer, mapping the unmappable, putting catalog numbers and provenance where once had been only waves and the profiles of sea serpents. Surely some people grieved for those sea serpents.

He didn't care. He kept at it, constructing his little monument to impermanence.

By March he was dating a sociology lecturer named Eileen, a no-nonsense young woman who made comforting, stodgy casseroles and gave him backrubs. He realized he would never know what his actual feelings for her were. She was not a girlfriend, she was a side effect of everything in the world that was Not Pamela. The house, too. Every now and then he thought, out of the blue, *But what did that woman mean, she bent over backwards for me?* And all day long, like a telegraph, he received the following message: *My wife has died, my wife has died, my wife has died.* Quieter than it had been: he could work over it now. He could act as though he were not an insane person with one single thought.

In April he got a tattoo at the downtown parlor where the students got theirs, a piece of paper wafting as though windswept over his bicep with a single word in black script: *Ephemera.*

Then it was May. His lease was over. Time to move again.

Through some spiritual perversity, he'd become fond of the house, its Sears, Roebuck feng shui, its square squatness, the way it got light all day long. Sally sent him e-mails, dithering over move-out dates, and for a full week threatened to renew the lease for a year. Would he be interested? He consulted his heart and was astounded to discover that, yes, he would. Finally she decided she would move back to the house on the first of June to get it ready to sell. Did he want to buy it? No, ma'am. Well, then: May 31.

He found an apartment with a bit of ocean view, a grown-up place with brand-new appliances and perfect arctic countertops that reminded him of no place: not the farmhouse in Normandy, or the beamed Roman apartment, or the thatched cottage near Odense. As he packed up the house he was relieved to see its former grubbiness assert itself, like cleaning an oil painting to find a murkier, uglier oil painting underneath. He noticed again the acoustic tiles on the upstairs ceilings and the blackness of the wooden floors. He took up the kilim in the living room and put down the old oriental; he packed his flat-screen TV, a splurge, into a box and found in the basement the old mammoth remoteless set and the hobbled particle-board cart. He cleaned the house as he'd never cleaned a rental before, because he was penitent and because he suspected Sally would use any opportunity to hold on to his security deposit; he washed walls and the insides of cupboards and baseboards and doorjambs. She had no idea how much work she had ahead of her, he thought. The old rocker was a pig to wrestle back into the house; he covered it with the Indian throw, so she would have someplace to sit, but he left the art off the walls, and he did not restock the kitchen.

And besides.

Besides, why should he?

Those boxes were time machines: if he even thought about them, all he could remember was the fury with which he packed them. These days he was pretending to be a nice, rational man.

He bought a bunch of daffodils and left them in a pickle

jar in the middle of the dining-room table with a note that reminded Sally of the location of her kitchenware and bed linens, and signed his name, and added his cell-phone number. Then he went away for the weekend, up the coast, so he could take a few days off from things, boxes, the fossil record of his life.

In the morning, the first cell-phone message was Sally, who wanted to know where her dishcloths were.

The second: bottom of the salad spinner.

The third: her birth certificate. She'd left it in the white desk that had been in the dining room, and where was that?

The fourth: what on earth had happened to the spices? Had he put them in a separate box?

The reception in this part of the state was miserable. He clamped the phone over one ear and his hand over the other.

"Sally?" he said.

She said, "Who's this?"

"Stony Badower."

There was silence.

"Your tenant—"

"I know," she said, in a grande dame voice. Then she sighed.

"Are you all right?" he asked.

"It's more daunting moving back in than I'd thought," she said.

"But you're all right."

"I found the dishcloths," she said. "And the desk."

"And the birth certificate?" he asked.

"Yes." More silence.

"Why don't I come over this evening when I get back," he said, "and I can—"

"Yes," she said. "That would be nice."

He'd imagined a woman who looked spun on a potter's wheel, round and glazed and built for neither beauty nor utility. Unbreakable till dropped from a height. Her daughter the small blonde gone to seed. But the door was answered by a woman as tall as him, 5'10", in her late sixties, more ironwork than pottery, with the dark hair and sharp nose of her granddaughter. She shook his hand. "Stony, hello." Over a flowered T-shirt she wore the sort of babyish bright-blue overalls that Berlin workmen favored, that no American grown-up, he had thought, would submit to. They showed off the alarmingly beautiful curve of her back as she retreated to the kitchen. Already she'd dug out some of the old pottery, and found a new tablecloth to cover the cigarette-burned oilcloth on the dining-room table.

"What I don't understand," she said. In each hand as she turned was a piece of a salad spinner: the lid with the cord that spun it like a gyroscope, the basket that turned. Her look described the anguish of the missing plastic bowl with the point at the bottom. His own salad spinner was waiting in a box in the new apartment. It worked by a crank.

"Who packed the kitchen?" she asked.

"I did," he said.

"What I don't understand," she said again, "was that these were in *separate* boxes. And the bottom? Gone."

"Oh," he said.

She gestured to the wooden shelf—Murphy-Oil-Soaped and bare—by the window. "What about the spices?"

"That's my fault," he said, though before he'd come over he'd Googled *how long keep spices* and was gratified by the answer. He could see them still, sticky, dusty, greenish brown grocery-store spice jars, the stubby plastic kind with the red tops. He'd thrown them out with everything else that had been half used. "I got rid of them. They were dirty. Everything in the kitchen was."

She shook her head sadly. "I wiped them all down in May."

"Sally," he said. "Really, I promise, the kitchen was dirty. It was so, so filthy." Was it? He tried to remember, envisioned the garbage can of flies, took heart. "Everything. It's possible that I didn't take time to pick out exactly what was clean and what wasn't, but that was how bad things were."

She sighed. "It's just—I thought I was moving back home."

"Oh," he said. "So—when did you move out?"

"Four years ago. When I retired. Sure. Carly grew up here, she didn't tell you? I was always very happy in this house."

"No," he said. He'd thought they'd moved ten years ago. Twenty.

"Listen, I have some favors to ask you. If you could help me move some furniture back in."

"Of course," he said.

"There's an armchair in the studio I'd like upstairs. So I have something to sit on. I was looking for my bed, you know. That really shouldn't have been moved."

"I said, I think—"

"It's all right. Amos made it. He made a lot of the furniture here—the shelves, the desks. He was a potter."

"I'm so sorry," he said, because after Pamela died, he promised himself that if anyone told him the smallest, saddest story, he would answer, *I'm so sorry*. Meaning, *Yes, that happened*. You couldn't believe the people who believed that not mentioning sadness was a kind of magic that could stave off the very sadness you didn't mention—as though grief were the opposite of Rumpelstiltskin and materialized only at the sound of its own name.

"That asshole," she said. "*Is* a potter, I should say." She looked around the kitchen. "It's just," she said. "The bareness. I wasn't expecting that."

She turned before his eyes from an iron widow into an abandoned wife. "I figured you were selling the house," he said.

She scratched the back of her neck. "Yes. Come," she said in the voice of a preschool teacher. "Studio."

It was raining, and so she put on a clear raincoat, another childish piece of clothing. She even belted it. They went out the back door that Stony had almost never used. In the rainy dusk, the transparent coat over the blue, she looked alternately like an art deco music box and a suburban sofa wrapped against spills.

The doorknob stuck. She pushed it with her hip. "Can

you?" she asked, and he manhandled it open and flicked on the light.

Here it was again: the table covered with pots, Picasso dancing, though now Picasso was covered up to his waist in mold. The smell was terrible. He saw the art he'd brought out nine months before, which he'd stacked carefully but no doubt had been destroyed by the damp anyhow. He felt the first flickers of guilt and tried to cover them with a few spadesful of anger: if it hadn't happened to her things, it would have happened to his.

"Here everything is," she said. She pointed in the corner. "Oh, I love that table. It was my mother's."

"Well, you said not the basement."

"You were here for only nine months," she said. She touched the edge of the desk that the blue pots sat on, and then turned and looked at him. "It's a lot to have done, for only nine months."

She was smiling then, beautifully. Raindrops ran tearfully down her plastic-covered bosom. She stroked them away and said, "When I walked in, it just felt as though the twenty-five years of our residency here had been erased."

O lady, he wanted to say, *you rented me a house, a house, not a museum devoted to you and to Laskeriana and the happiness and failure of your marriage. You charged me market rent, and I paid it so I could* live *somewhere*. But he realized he'd gotten everything wrong. She had not left her worst things behind four years ago, but her best things, her beloved things, she'd left the art hoping it brought beauty into the lives of the students and summer renters and way-

ward other subletters, all those people unfortunate enough
not to have made a home yet. She loved the terra-cotta sun
that he'd taken down from the kitchen the first day. She
loved the bed made for her in the 1970s by that clever,
wretched man, her husband. She bought herself a cheap
salad spinner so her tenants could use this one that worked
so well. If Pamela had been with him that day nine months
ago, she would have known. She would have seen the pieces
of key chain and clucked over the dirty rug and told him the
whole story. This was a house abandoned by sadness, not a
war or epidemic but the end of a marriage, and kept in place
to commemorate both the marriage and its ruin.

"It was such a strange feeling, to see everything gone,"
she said. "As though ransacked. You know?"

He'd never even called the French landlord to ask about
Trudy the lusterware duck, and right now that seemed like
the biggest lack in his life, worse than Pamela, who he knew
to be no longer on this earth. He should have carried the
duck to America, though he'd scattered Pamela's ashes on
the broads in Norfolk. He should have flown to Bremen,
where she was from, to startle her mother and sisters, demanded to see her childhood bed, tracked it down if it was
gone to whatever thrift store or relative it had been sent
to—Pamela was the one who taught him that a bed on dis-
play is never just furniture, it is a spirit portrait of everyone
who has ever slept in it, been born in it, had sex in it, died
in it. *Look,* she said. *You can see them if you look.* He had
done everything wrong.

"I know," he said. "I'm sorry," he said, and then, "It was
already broken."

Some Terpsichore

1.

There's a handsaw hanging on the wall of my living room, a house key from a giant's pocket. It's been there a long time. "What's your saw for?" people ask, and I say, "It's not my saw. I never owned a saw."

"But what's it *for*?"

"Hanging," I answer.

By now if you took it down you'd see the ghost of the saw behind. Or—no, not the ghost, because the blue wallpaper would be dark where the saw had protected it from the sun. Ghosts are pale. So the room is the ghost. The saw is the only thing that's real.

These days, though it grieves me to say it, that sounds about right.

2.

Here's how I became a singer. Forty years ago I walked past the Washington Monument in Baltimore and thought, *I'll climb that*. It was first thing in the morning. They'd just opened up. As I climbed I sang with my eyes closed— "Summertime," I think it was. Yes, of course it was. "Summertime." I kept my hand on the iron banister. My feet found the stairs. In my head I saw myself at a party, leaning on a piano, singing in front of a small audience. I climbed, I sang. I never could remember the words, largely because of a spoonerized version my friend Fred liked to sing— *Tummersime, and the iving is leazy / jif are fumping, and the hiver is rye . . .*

Then a man's voice said, "Wow."

In my memory, he leans against the wall two steps from the top, shouldering a saw like a rifle. But of course he wouldn't have brought his saw to the Washington Monument. He was a big-boned, raw-faced blond man with a smashed Parker House roll of a nose, a puny felt hat hanging on the back of his head. His slacks were dark synthetic, snagged. His orange cardigan looked like rusted Brillo. He was so big you wondered how he could have got up there— had the tower been built around him? Had he arrived in pieces and been assembled on the spot? "Wow," he said again, and clasped his hands in front of himself, bouncing on his knees with the syncopated jollification of a lovestruck 1930s cartoon character. I expected to see querulous lines of excitement coming off his head, punctuated by exclamation marks. He plucked off his hat. His hair looked like it had been combed with a piece of buttered toast.

"That was you?" he asked.

I nodded. Maybe he was some municipal employee, charged with keeping the noise down.

"You sound like a saw," he said. His voice was soft. I thought he might be from the South, like me, though later I found out he just had one of those voices that picked up accents through static electricity. Really he was from Paterson, New Jersey.

"A saw?" I asked.

He nodded.

I put my fingers to my throat. "I don't know what that means."

He held up his big hands, one still palming his hat. *"Beautiful,"* he said. "Not of this earth. Come with me, I'll show you. Boy, you sure taught George Gershwin a lesson. Where do you sing?"

"Nowhere," I said.

I couldn't sing, according to my friends. The only person who'd ever said anything nice about my voice was my friend Fred Tibbets, who claimed that when I was drunk, sometimes I managed to carry a tune. But we drank a lot in those days, and when I was drunk Fred was drunk, too, and sentimental. Still, I secretly believed I could sing. My only evidence was the pleasure singing brought me. Most common mistake in the world, believing that physical pleasure and virtue are in any way related, directly or indirectly.

The man shook his head. "No good," he said very seriously. "That's rotten. We'll change that." He went to take my hand and instead hung his hat upon it. Then I felt his own hand squeeze mine through the felt. "You'll sing for me, OK? Would you sing for me? You'll sing for me."

He led me back down the monument, the hat on my hand, his hand behind it. My wrist began to sweat but I didn't mind. "Of course you'll sing," he said. He went ahead of me but kept stopping, so I'd half tumble onto the point of his elbow. "I know people. I'm from Philadelphia. Well, I live there. I came to Bawlmore because a buddy of mine, part of a trio, he broke his arm and needed a guitar player so there you go. There are two hundred and twenty-eight steps on this thing. I read it on the plaque. Also I counted. God, you're a skinny girl, you're like *nothing*, you're so lovely, no, you are, don't disagree, I know what I'm talking about. Well, not all the time, but right now I do. I'll play you my saw. Not everyone appreciates it but you will. What's your name? Once more? Oof. We'll change that, have to, you need something short and to the point. Take me, I used to be Gabriel McClonnahashem, there's a moniker, huh? Now I'm Gabe Macon. For you, I don't know, let me think: Miss Porth. Because you're a chanteuse, that's why the Miss. And Porthkiss, I don't know. And Miss Kiss is just silly. Look at you blush! The human musical saw. There are all sorts of places you can sing, you don't know your own worth, that's your problem. I've known singers and I've known singers. I heard you and I thought, *There's a voice I could listen to for the rest of my life*. I'm not kidding. I don't kid about things like that. I don't kid about music. I was frozen to the spot. Look, still: goose bumps.

You rescued me from the tower, Rapunzel: I climbed down on your voice. I'll talk to my friend Jake. I'll talk to this other guy I know. I have a feeling about you. I have a *feeling* about you. Are you getting as dizzy as me? Maybe it's not the stairs. Do you believe in love at first sight? That's not a line, it's a question. I do, of course I do, would I ask if I didn't? Because I believe in luck, that's why. We're nearly at the bottom. Poor kid, you never even got to the top. Come on. For ten cents it's strictly an all-you-can-climb monument. We'll go back up. Come on. Come on."

"I can sing?" I asked him.

He looked at me. His eyes were green, with gears of darker green around the pupils.

"Trust me," he said.

3.

I wasn't the sort of girl who'd climb a monument with a strange man. Or go back to his hotel room with him. Or agree to move to Philadelphia the next day.

But I did.

His room was on the top floor of the Elite Hotel, the kind of place you might check in to to commit suicide: toilet down the hall, a sink in the corner of the room, a view of another building with windows exactly across from the Elite's windows.

"Musical saw," said Gabe Macon. He opened a cardboard suitcase that sat at the end of the single bed. First he took out a long item wrapped in a sheet. A violin bow. Then a piece of rosin.

"You hit it with that?" I asked.

"Hit it? What hit?" Gabe said.

"I thought—"

"Look," he said. The saw he'd hung in the closet with his suits. I'd thought a musical saw would be a percussion instrument. A xylophone, maybe. A marimba. He rosined the bow and sat on a chair on the corner. The saw was just a regular wood saw. He clamped his feet on the end of it and then pulled the bow across the dull side of the blade. You could hardly see the saw, the handle clamped between his feet, the end of the metal snagged in his hand: he was a pile of man with a blade at the heart, a man doing violence to something with an unlikely weapon.

It was the voice of a beautiful toothache. It was the sound of every enchanted harp, flute, princess turned into a tree in every fairy tale ever written.

"I sound like that?" I said.

He nodded, kept playing.

I sound like that. It was humiliating, alarming, ugly, exciting. It was like looking at a flattering picture of yourself doing something you wished you hadn't been photographed doing. *That's me.* He was playing "Fly Me to the Moon."

He finished and looked at me with those Rube-Goldberg eyes. "That's you," he said. He flexed the saw back and forth then dropped it to the ground.

I picked it up and tried to see my reflection in the metal. "You don't take the teeth off?"

"Nope," he said. "This is my second saw. Here. Give me." I lifted it by the blade and he caught it through the tawny handle. "First one I bought was too good. Short, expensive. Wouldn't bend. You need something cheap and with a good length to it. Eight points to an inch, this one. Teeth, I mean." He flexed it. The metal made that back-stage thunder noise I'd imagined when he'd first said I sounded like a saw. "This one, though. It's right." He flipped it around and caught it again between his brown shoes and drew the bow against it. He'd turned on just one light by the hotel bed when we'd come into the room. Now it was dark out. I listened to the saw and looked at the sink in the corner. A spider crawled out of it, tapping one leg in front musingly like a blind man with a cane before clamber-ing over the embankment. The saw sighed. Me, too. Then Gabe reached over with the bow and touched my shoulder. I flinched, as though the horsehair had caught a case of sharp off the saw.

"That's you," he said again.

Maybe I loved Gabe already. What's love at first sight but a bucket thrown over you that smoothes out all your previ-ous self-loathing, so that you can see yourself slick and matted down and audacious? At least, I believed for the first time that I was capable of being loved.

Or maybe I just loved the saw.

4.

We left for Philly the next day. The story of our success, and it wasn't much success, is pretty boring, as all such stories are. A lot of waiting by the phone. A lot of bad talent nights. One great talent night in which I won a box of dishes. The walk home from that night, Gabe carrying the dishes and smashing them into the gutter one by one. *Don't do it,* I said, *those are mine—*

He held one dish to my forehead, then lifted it up, then touched it down again, the way you do with a hammer to a nail before you drive it in.

Then he stroked my forehead with the plate edge.

"Don't tell me what to do," he said.

5.

He wrote songs. Before I met him I had no idea of how anyone wrote a song. His apartment on Sansom Street smelled of burnt tomato sauce and had in the kitchen, in place of a stove, a piano that looked as though it had been through a house fire. Sometimes he played it. Sometimes he sat at it with his hands twitching over the keys like leashed dogs. "The Land Beyond the Land We Know." "A Pocket Full of Pennies." "Your Second Biggest Regret." "Keep Your Eyes Out for Me." He was such a sly mimic, such a sneaky thief, that people thought these were obscure standards, if such a thing exists, songs they'd heard many times long ago and were only now remembering. He wrote a song every day. He got mad that sometimes I couldn't keep them straight or remember them all. "That's a Hanging Offense." "Don't You Care at All." "Till the End of Us."

We performed them together. He bought me a green Grecian-draped dress that itched, and matching opera gloves that were too long and cut into my armpits, and lipstick, and false eyelashes—all haunted, especially the eyelashes.

History is full of the sad stories of foolish women. What's terrible is that I was not foolish. Ask anyone. Ask Fred Tibbets, who lied and said I could carry a tune.

We cut a record called *Miss Porth Sings!* For a long time you could still find it in bins in record shops under *Vocals* or *Other* or *Novelty*. Me on the sleeve, my head tipped back. I wore red lipstick that made my complexion orange, and tiny saw-shaped earrings. My hair was cashew-colored.

That was a fault of the printing. In real life, in those days, my hair was the color of sandpaper: diamond, garnet, ruby.

I was on the radio. I was on the *Gypsy Rose Lee Show.* Miss Porth, the Human Musical Saw! But the whole point was that Gabe's saw sounded human. Why be a human who only sounds like an inanimate object that sounds human?

6.

This is not a story about success. In the world we were what we'd always been. The love story: the saw and the sawish voice. We were two cripplingly shy, witheringly judgmental people who fell in love in private, away from the conversation and caution of other people, and then we left town before anyone could warn us.

In Philadelphia he began to throw things at me—silly, embarrassing, lighter-than-air things: a bowl full of egg whites I was about to whip for a soufflé, my brother's birthday card, the entire contents of a newly opened box of powdered sugar. For days I left white fingerprints behind.

He said it was an accident, he hadn't meant to throw it at all. He was only gesturing.

And then he began to threaten me with the saw.

I don't think he could have explained it himself. He didn't drink, but he would seem drunk. The drunkenness, or whatever it was, moved his limbs. Picked up the saw. Brought it to my throat, and just held it there. He never moved the blade, and spoke of the terrible things he would do to himself.

"I'm going to commit suicide," he said. "I will. Don't leave me. Tell me you won't."

I couldn't shake my head or speak, and so I tried to look at him with love. I couldn't stand the way he hated himself. I wanted to kill the person who made him feel this way. Our apartment was bright at the front, by the windows, and black and airless at the back, where the bed was. Where we were now, lying on a quilt that looked like a classroom map, orange, blue, green, yellow.

"My life is over," said Gabe. He had the burnt-tomato smell of the whole apartment. "I'm old. I'm old. I'm talentless. I can see it, but you know, at the same time, I listen to the radio all day and I don't understand. Why will you break everyone's hearts the way you do? Why do you do it? You're crazy. Probably you're not capable of love. You need help. I will kill myself. I've thought about it ever since I was a little kid."

The saw blade took a bite of me, eight tooth marks per inch. Cheap steel, the kind that bent easily. I had my hands at the dull side of the saw. *How did we get here,* I wondered, but I'd had the same disoriented thought when I believed I'd fallen in love with him at first sight, lying in the same bed: *How did this happen?*

"I could jump," he said. "What do you think I was doing up that tower when you found me? Windows were too small, I didn't realize. I'd gotten my nerve up. But then there you were, and you were so little. And your voice. And I guess I changed my mind. Will you say something, Marya? You've broken my heart. One of these days I'll kill myself."

I knew everything about him. He weighed exactly twice what I did, to the pound. He was ambitious and doubtful: he wanted to be famous, and he wanted no one to look at him, ever, which is probably the human condition—in him it was merely amplified. That was nearly all I knew about him. Sometimes we still told the story of our life together to each other: Why had I climbed the tower *that* day? Why had he? He had almost stayed in Philadelphia. I'd almost gone back home for the weekend but then my great-aunt Florence died and my folks went to her funeral. If he'd been five minutes slower he wouldn't have caught me singing. If I'd been ten minutes later, I would have smiled at him as he left.

We were lucky, we told each other, blind pure luck.

7.

One night we were at our standing gig, at a cabaret called Maxie's. It hurt to sing, with the pearls sticking to the saw cuts. The owner was named Marco Bell. He loved me. Marco's face was so wrinkled that when he smoked you could see every line in his face tense and slacken.

> *There's a land beyond the land we know,*
> *Where time is green and men are slow.*
> *Follow me and soon you'll know,*
> *Blue happiness.*

My green dress was too big and I kept having to hitch it up. It wasn't too big a month ago. At the break, I sat down next to Marco. "How are you?" I asked.

"Full of sorrow," he answered. He leaned into the hand holding the cigarette. I thought he might light his pomaded hair on fire.

"I'm sorry," I said.

"*You* do it, Miss Porth. With your—" He waved at the spot where I'd been standing.

I laughed. "They're not all sad songs."

"Yes," he said. There was not a joke in a five-mile radius of the man. He had a great Russian head with bullying eyebrows. Three years earlier his wife had had a stroke, and sometimes she came into the club in a chevron-patterned dress, sitting in her wheelchair and patting the tabletop, either in time to the music or looking for something she'd put down there. "You're wrong. They are."

I said, "Sometimes I don't think I'm doing anyone any favors."

Then Gabe was behind me. He touched my shoulder lovingly. Listen: don't tell me otherwise. It was not nice love, it was not good love, but you cannot tell me that it wasn't love. Love is not oxygen, though many songwriters will tell you that it is; it is not a chemical substance that is either definitively present or absent; it cannot be reduced to its parts. It is not like a flower, or an animal, or anything that you will ever be able to recognize when you see it. Love is food. That's all. Neither better nor worse. Sometimes very good. Sometimes terrible. But to say—as people will—*that wasn't love*. As though that makes you feel better! Well, it might not have been nourishing, but it sustained me for a while. Once I'd left I'd be as bad as any reformed sinner, amazed at my old self, but even with the blade against my neck, I loved him, his worries about the future, his reliable black moods, his reliable affection—that was still there, too, though sullied by remorse.

I stayed for the saw, too. Not the threat of it. I stayed because of those minutes on stage when I could understand it. Gabe bent it back and it called out, *Oh, no, honey, help.* It wanted comfort. It wanted to comfort me. We were in trouble together, the two of us: the honey-throated saw, the saw-voiced girl. *Help, help, we're still alive,* the saw sang, though mostly its songs were just pronouns all stuck together: *I, we, mine, you, you, we, mine.*

Yes, that's right. I was going to tell you about the saw.

Gabe touched my shoulder and said, "Marya, let's go."

Marco said, "In a minute. Miss Porth, let's have a drink."

"Marya," said Gabe.

"I'd love one," I said.

Maxie's was a popular place—no sign on the front door, a private joke. There was a crowd. Gabe punched me. He punched me in the breast. The right breast. A very strange place to take a punch. Not the worst place. I thought that as it happened: *not the worst place to take a punch*. The chairs at Maxie's had backs carved like bamboo. He punched me. I'd never been punched before. He said, "See how it feels, when someone breaks your heart?" and I thought, *Yes, as it happens, I think I do*.

I was on my back. Marco had his arms around Gabe's arms and was whispering things in his ear. A crowd had formed. People were touching me. I wished they wouldn't.

Here is what I want to tell you: I knew something was ending, and I was grateful, and I missed it.

8.

About five years ago in a restaurant near my apartment someone recognized me. "You're—are you Miss Porth?" he said. "You're Miss Porth." Man about my own age, tweed blazer, bald with a crinkly snub-nosed puppyish face, the kind that always looks like it's about to sneeze. "I used to see you at Maxie's," he said. "All the time. Well, lots. I was in grad school at Penn. Miss Porth! Good God! I always wondered what happened to you!"

I was sitting at the bar, waiting for a friend, and I wanted to end the conversation before the friend arrived. The man took a bar stool next to me. We talked for a while about Philadelphia. He still lived there, he was just in town for a conference. He shook the ice from his emptied drink into his mouth, and I knew he was back there—not listening to me, exactly, just remembering who was at his elbow, and did she want another drink, and did he have enough money for another drink for both of them. All the good things he believed about himself then: by now he'd know whether he'd been right, and right or wrong, knowing was dull. I didn't like being his occasion for nostalgia.

"I have your album," he said. "I'm a fan. Seriously. It's my field, music. I— Some guy hit you," he said suddenly. His puppy face looked over-sneezeish. "I can't remember. Was he a drunk? Some guy in love with you? That's right. A crazy."

"Random thing," I said. "What were you studying?"

"Folklore," he said absentmindedly. "I always wondered something about you. Can I ask? Do you mind?"

Oh, I thought, *slide down that rabbit hole if you have to, just let go of my hem, don't take me with you.*

"I loved to hear you," he said. Puppy tilt to his head, too. "You were like nothing else. But I always wondered—I mean, you seem like an intelligent woman. I never spoke to you back then." One piece of ice clung to the bottom of his glass and he fished it out with his fingers. "Did you realize that people were laughing at you?"

Then he said, "Oh, my God."

"I'm sorry," he said.

"Not me," he said. "I swear, you were wonderful."

I turned to him. "Of course I knew," I said. "How could I miss it?"

The line between pride and a lack of it is thin and brittle and thrilling as new ice. Only when you're young are you able to skate out onto it, to not care which side you end up on. That was me. I was innocent. Later, when you're old, when you know things, well, it takes all sorts of effort, and ropes, and pulleys, and all kinds of tricks, to keep you from crashing through, if you're even willing to risk it.

Though maybe I did know back then that some people didn't take me seriously. But still: the first time they came to laugh. Not the second. I could hear the audience. I could hear how still they were when I sang with my eyes closed. Sure, some of them had thought, *Who does she think she's fooling? Who does she think she is, with that old green gown, with those made-up songs?* But then they'd listen. It was those people, I think, the ones who thought at first they were above me, who got the wind knocked out of them. Who brought their friends the next week. Who bought my record. Who thought: *Me. No more, no less, she's fooling me.*

Later I got a letter asking for the right to put two songs from *Miss Porth Sings!* on a record called *Songs from Mars: Eccentrics and their Music.* The note said, *Do you know what happened to G. Macon? I need his permission, too, of course.*

9.

The night of the punch, I went home with Gabe for the last time. *Of course, don't call the police,* I told Marco. He was exhausted, repentant. I led him to the bed, to the faded quilt, and he fell asleep. From the kitchen phone I called his sister in Paterson, whom I'd never met, and I told her Gabe Macon was in trouble and alone and needed help. Then I climbed into bed next to him. Gabe had an archipelago of moles on his neck I'd never noticed, and a few faint acne scars on his nose. His eyebrows were knit in dreamy thought. I loved that nose. He hated it. "Do I really look like that?" he'd ask, seeing a picture of himself. He'd cover his nose with his hand.

I didn't know what would become of him. I had to quit caring. It wasn't love and it wasn't the saw and it wasn't a fear of being alone that kept me there: it was wanting to know the end of the story, and wanting the end to be happy.

At five A.M. I left with a bag, the saw, bamboo-patterned bruises on my back, and a fist-shaped bruise on my right breast. Soon enough I was amazed at how little I cared for him. Maybe that was worse than anything.

10.

Still, no matter what, I can't shake my first impression. Even now, miles and years away, the saw in my living room to remind me, when I think of Gabe, I see a 1930s animated character: the black pie-cut eyes, white gloved hands held flat against the background, dark long limbs without elbows and knees that do not bend but undulate. The cheap jazzy glorious music that, despite your better self, puts you in a good mood. Fills you with cheap jazzy hope. And it seems you're making big strides across the country on your spring-operated limbs, in your spring-loaded open car, in your jazzy pneumatic existence. You don't even notice that behind you, over and over in the same order, is the same tree, shack, street corner, mouse hole, table set for dinner, blown-back curtains.

Juliet

We called the bunny that lived in the children's room Kaspar, as in Kaspar Hauser, but the children who came to torment and visit it thought we meant the friendly ghost. That might have made sense had the rabbit been white, but it was dun-colored. It cowered in the corner of its cage while children stuck their fingers through the wire; they sang, *Bunny, bunny, bunny rabbit;* they cried when their mothers informed them it was time to go, they'd see Bunny next time. Bunny, we suspected, prayed nightly to become a ghost. It never got out, never saw sunlight; it was never given a carrot or a chance to hop; it indulged in no lapine pleasures at all. Mostly, it shook or slept, was careless about its hygiene. Mornings, it ripped its newsprint bedding in strips and drew them into its mouth in damp pleats, chewing and swallowing by inches. The children's librarian said this was normal, but we thought the bunny was trying to overdose, using the materials nearby.

The six finches, on the other hand, seemed happy in their communal cage; and if the fish were unhappy, we couldn't tell. Maybe they wept in the terrible privacy of their tank. The occasional dog would slip in through the exit, wanting to find its owner, and one woman brought her cat, left it crying like a baby in the vestibule while she returned a video. "I am in a hurry," she told the circulation desk. "My cat is waiting for me." Also, once, a man found a wounded bird outside the library and brought it to the reference desk for identification. When he opened his hand to indicate the peculiarities of its markings, the bird took a notion to live after all and flew to the highest corner of the balcony, up by the replica Parthenon frieze that girdled the reading room. The bird stayed there for days, setting off the motion detectors at night. It never got close enough to the reference desk to identify.

That was it for wildlife, unless you counted the children themselves, often wild: not the toddlers, who couldn't bear to leave the bunny's side, but the ten- and eleven-year-olds who threw books off the balcony or slung their skinny legs on the tables or slipped whatever they wished, like a bad joke, into the book drop. The book drop was a door set in the library façade that opened like an oven and dropped its contents into a closet in the circulation office. Snow in the winter, firecrackers in the summer, uncapped bottles of Coke year-round. One weekend, a passing man employed the book drop for a public urinal, and several books were destroyed. "Urine is sterile," the head of circulation explained to her staff as she dropped a sodden *Garfield Rounds Out* into a wastebasket, but it was clear nobody believed this perfectly scientific fact, including her.

It was on this day, a Monday, that we first saw Juliet.

She was a young woman, late twenties we thought, with long, loose dark hair. Her clothes were white, and at first we thought she was in uniform, a nurse, perhaps—she had a sort of nursey look to her, sweet and determined and recently divorced. Or maybe she was from an unfamiliar order of nuns, because in our library we did get the occasional Sister. But it turned out she just wore white that day. Maybe she wasn't wearing white, maybe we just remember that now because in the picture we saw so often, later, she wore white. At any rate, there was something forsaken and hopeful about her. She stood patiently at the front desk, waiting for assistance. In front of her, a man filled out an application for a card. On the line marked OCCUPATION, he filled in EMPLOYEE.

She clutched a book in her hand in such a way that it looked like a knife she was prepared to use on herself, which was one of the reasons we ended up calling her Juliet. That, and her habit of leaning on the rail of the balcony that ran around the reading room, looking up instead of down, into the cloudy green of the skylight. Her book had that pebbly leatherette navy-blue grain usually found on diaries and giveaway Bibles. *Are you returning that?* somebody asked her.

"No," she said. "No. It's mine. I just was never in here before, and I was wondering what you could tell me."

The departments were pointed out to her—audiovisual this way, children's the other, adult library upstairs. She was offered a brochure.

"May I get a card?"

Was she a resident of the town? Yes. Had she had a card with us before? No. Did she have proof of address and a photo ID?

"Not with me," she said. "Next time, then. For now, I'll just look around."

We had regulars, of course, and they were demanding. People wanted not just books but attention and advice and, in the case of one widower, the occasional rear end to pat affectionately. We got teenagers who came daily to read or nap or use the Internet away from their parents; mothers and their toddlers and their tiny trails of cheese crackers. We had two transgendered patrons that we knew of, one now a radical lesbian who came in with her girlfriend and wore a T-shirt that said, BECAUSE I'M THE TOP, THAT'S WHY, who liked to gab and gossip; the other the shy and girlish and bangled Janice, whom we'd first known as Jonathan, winner three years in a row of the junior high science fair, under both names one of our most regular regulars. There was a woman with no eyebrows who never said a word and a pleasant, paranoid old lady who occasionally, sweetly, accused us of poisoning her. There were the screamers, mostly businessmen who believed they could threaten our jobs and could not understand why we humble city employees weren't frightened. One blond man—his face as ruddy and pitted as a basketball—screamed, "Where's the guy who wouldn't let my son take out books?" The guy in question was outside, obliviously smoking a cigarette, and though the matter was resolved, clearly what the man really wanted was to punch someone.

The man's son, who looked just like him, though with a beautiful complexion, hadn't seemed at all disturbed or surprised by the delinquency of his library card. He was a quiet kid who had to lick his lips several times to get his mouth to work, and then he'd said only, "OK." It turned out he'd been checking out books for his grandfather, anyhow; the clerk at the desk told his father the kid should just bring in his grandfather's card.

We got asked for love advice and job applications, the whereabouts of relatives. "Did you see a girl?" a kid would ask, and the head of circulation would answer wearily, "I've seen lots of girls." One man called because he wanted to know whether his daughter, whom he had not seen in five years, had a library card she'd used recently.

"I'd like to see her again," he said when he was told library records were confidential. "I think maybe she tried to contact me a few years ago."

When somebody like this called—for instance, the woman who wanted to know how to stop having bad thoughts—the circulation desk happily sent the person to reference, because, after all, it sounded like a job for a professional librarian.

Juliet surprised us, coming back every day, clean, starched. Usually, the people who showed up like that looked slightly worse every visit. She never did get that library card, but many of our most beloved patrons never did. She favored the children's room. She became special friends with the children's librarian, a young woman who said everything as if she were reading a story, as if the end of her sentence contained a wonderful surprise: a beggar revealed to be a lost prince, a talkative young bear no longer afraid of the dark. The children's librarian had no friends at the library. She wore peasant skirts and thick-soled shoes and pendants on long black strings. Juliet smiled, listened to the librarian's stories, consoled her the day the Harriet Tubman impersonator failed to show up for the Black History Month program. Once a week, they ate lunch together in the park in front of the building, at one of the concrete tables with an inlaid chessboard. Frequently, Juliet talked to the rabbit. The bunny eyed her with its usual unhappiness, another grubby pair of hands reaching into the cage. Human flesh gave our neurotic bunny the willies.

In this the rabbit was not so different from the head of reference, who had been cranky for so long his bad mood had turned to superstition, a primitive who believed that the requests for addresses and statistics from the reference collection were akin to soul stealing. He was particularly suspicious of Juliet. Too sunny, that one, and the way she said hello, every single time: she wanted something. She was formulating an immense, subtly impossible, demanding, deadly reference question, one that would begin in the almanacs kept at the desk and then lead to encyclopedias, newspaper articles, and finally some now-unknown reference book kept in the basement, some cursed volume that turned its opener to dust. Even then, there would be no answer.

"I don't trust her," said the head of reference. "She wants something."

The other librarians bumped into one another behind the reference desk, trying to intercept patrons before they got to the head of reference, who claimed to be ignorant of any subject that sounded vaguely scientific.

We heard the big news slowly. There had been a murder. A woman. A woman from our town, killed in her own house. A woman stabbed ten times, twenty, sixty-three. It was as if the police were taking forever to examine the body and called up the local gossips to report: we found five more wounds in the last hour. You could see the cops, turning the body over and over, looking for what was neither evidence nor cause of death—she'd died after her poor body had caught the knife only a few times—one officer with a pencil and white pad, making hash marks. The final count was ninety-six.

A murder. We hoped for two things: that we did not know the victim and that the murderer did. *Please,* we prayed, though we never said those prayers aloud, *let it be a husband, a boyfriend.* We wanted to read in the paper: *Last week, she filed for a restraining order.* Hadn't every murdered woman? None of the library staff had ever asked for a restraining order, except the assistant director, who'd filed one against his sister. That was entirely different.

And then, on the evening news, we saw her picture: Juliet.

It wasn't the usual blurry victim snapshot, the kind that

makes it seem as if the last thing the person did, before hauling off and getting killed, was to indulge an elderly uncle with a camera. Juliet's picture—the one that appeared on all the newscasts, on the covers of all the papers—was clear and sharp and pretty. Her hair was done. She was wearing a white strapless gown. Depending on how the paper or channel cropped the picture, you could see the shoulder of her date, wearing a white jacket and black bow tie. He was still alive; you didn't need to see any more of him. He wasn't a suspect.

Her name was Suzanne Cunningham. She was thirty-four. She was, in fact, divorced (we'd suspected) and had three children (we'd had no idea). The oldest, a boy, was fifteen; the two girls were twelve and thirteen. The children's librarian had known all of this, of course, but would not answer questions. In fact, she had taken several days off work around the time of the murder, and we made a few dark jokes about how suspicious that seemed. Oh, that sweetness and light and arts-and-crafts stuff, that didn't fool us. She must be a sadist. Look how she treats that poor rabbit.

We didn't believe our jokes, but we needed them. Our town was near a big city, but it wasn't the big city. The famous names of murderers and murdered women—they often shared the same name, of course—were featured in the metropolitan paper, not ours. We had never seen the faces close up or walked by the houses.

The only thing the children's librarian said, when she came in to ask the director for the rest of the week off, was, *She knew. She knew someone was after her.*

One of the reference librarians confirmed it: Suzanne Cunningham had once asked for a book that would tell her how to keep people out of her house. *Burglars?* the librarian had asked. *Anyone*, Suzanne Cunningham answered. *I think someone has been sneaking into my house.* So the librarian had found a crime-prevention book, which Suzanne Cunningham smiled at and set down on a table without reading.

That made us feel better—a boyfriend, surely, or even her ex-husband—but we wondered why the newspapers didn't say so. The book she carried: it must be a diary—it must have clues. We wondered why she hadn't called the police. Someone sneaks into your house, you have to be worried, don't you?

Maybe not. Maybe you don't know that someone has been there—you just suspect. Nothing is broken or rearranged; no pets have been menaced. There's just the lingering, careless presence of someone who doesn't know how the house works. The back door has to be closed with both a knee and a shoulder; the kitchen faucets must be turned off with a wrench; mud must be knocked from shoes and the portable phone doesn't always want to hang up and the fridge door will float open if you aren't careful. And then one day, when the kids are with their father—thank God, as it turns out—you come home and surprise him in your kitchen. Maybe you've known all along who it was.

And maybe he even has a crush on you. That's the thing about crushes—sometimes they fly below the radar, the way in high school, when someone told you a boy had a crush, you could tell by the way he ignored you. The way he ignored you meant everything. A terrible word, crush—you could die from crushing, from having one, anyhow; you remember listening to music that meant the world to you and nothing, you were quite sure, to your beloved. Who knows what teenagers listen to today; your own boy plays music that you can't imagine swooning to; your own boy is friends with this boy, who is now in your kitchen, licking his lips nervously to oil up his mouth. You know everything about this kid: a neighborhood babysitter, sixteen years old but enormous, big enough to gently swing a laughing five-year-old over his head without fear; an altar boy who goes to the library to pick up books for his grandfather, in his pocket the grandfather's faultless library card; a part-time drugstore clerk; a good boy who loves his parents, whose parents love him.

What you don't know is that he has a knife, and that you have frightened him.

Ninety-six times, though. We couldn't imagine it. We tried it ourselves, started to hit our own knees softly, ninety-six times. We gave up, we got tired, we made ourselves sick.

Four days later, they made the arrest. The accused was the blond boy whose father had come in screaming. Another library patron. We all knew him, too: Tommy Mason. The Masons were a big, famous family in our town. Tommy Mason's grandfather had been mayor once, back in the 1950s.

An altar boy, a good boy, a boy with a library card. Could such a boy possibly be guilty? He lived across the street from the dead woman. He had shoveled her walk in the winter; his sisters had sold her Girl Scout cookies. He was good friends with Suzanne Cunningham's oldest child, Kevin. Kevin Cunningham had found his mother's body.

Within twenty-four hours, every library staff member who knew how had looked up the accused's library record. Tommy Mason's card was still delinquent, told us nothing: a single book called *Soap Science,* no doubt for school. We looked at the record for the book daily—the title, the author (Bell), the publication date (1993), the due date (May 4, two years ago). We wanted to know something. These were the only facts we had.

We weren't supposed to do that, of course. We were supposed to be bound by ethics and privacy, but it felt as if we could break them, the way that cannibalism, in certain extreme cases, is acceptable.

He was put in jail, and nothing could persuade the judge—also a patron, as it happened—to let him out on bail. Reports came down from the neighborhood and on the TV news. Mr. and Mrs. Mason let themselves be interviewed in their kitchen. They swore that it was impossible, that time would prove them right. Ask anyone in the neighborhood: Tom was the best kid. He wasn't even interested in girls—why would he kill one? The Masons' hands were woven together on the kitchen tabletop; their fingers were the same pink, their hands a solid knot. Mr. Mason was calm and reasonable. We wondered whether Tommy Mason was taking the fall for him. We remembered the screaming father, bright red with the idea we'd denied Tommy Mason anything; surely he turned that anger on his family.

The papers interviewed neighbors. *Such a nice boy. There was something about him. He didn't have a temper.*

You know, he was off—he didn't have what you'd call emo-
tions. He was shy. He was a loner. He was a daydreamer.
Sometimes he stared through people's windows.

Really, there was no prior proof other than vague gossip.
He really was, or had been, a good kid, and who knew? The
book Juliet had carried was discovered in her living room;
it contained only sketches of her children. Maybe Tommy
Mason's parents—and some of the people on the street,
who'd already lost one neighbor—were right. Maybe
Tommy Mason was innocent and the two men he said he'd
seen fleeing the scene were at large, dreaming of their perfect crime. A single perfect crime: the woman was not
raped, the house was not robbed, the door had not been
tampered with.

There were two bloody fingerprints, Tommy Mason's,
in the cellar. Bloody, but not his blood. The police said that,
and we believed them.

Tommy Mason stayed in jail, and people stopped believing he hadn't done it. Of course he'd done it. TV re-
porters were no longer interested in his parents' version of
the story. One day, at a community picnic in the park, a
Little League coach began his remarks, "With all the trou-
bles in our neighborhood in past months . . ." and one of
Tommy Mason's sisters was there. She went home to tell
Mrs. Mason, who returned and stood at the edge of the
baseball field. Mrs. Mason was a small woman to have had
such a big son, and she looked smaller, cut into diamonds
by the chain link of the backstop. "You'll be sorry!" she
screamed. She curled her fingers into the fence. "You'll see,
my Tommy never did it! You'll see, you assholes!" Some

people wondered whether they should go to her, say something comforting. But she scared them, rattling the backstop. Maybe she'd start climbing up it. People walked the other way. They waited for her to stop.

And perhaps she never will stop. What can you do? Your son, your only boy—whether he killed somebody or not, though he didn't—is lost to you. He never could have killed anyone. He never even liked horror movies. He was always respectful. He believes in God. And if—though he didn't!—if he did kill her, that's one life gone already. Your child used to live in your house, and he has been taken from you, and all you can hope for is that eventually he will be returned. He will already be ruined. The best you can hope for is your ruined boy back in your house.

Tommy Mason—no matter what—has no doubt already been ruined. The newspapers refer to the Tommy Mason Case, not the Suzanne Cunningham Murder. In fifty years, neighborhood kids will choose kickball teams with rhymes about Tommy Mason, not knowing exactly who that was. Tommy Mason had a knife / Tommy Mason took a life / How. Many. Times. Did. He. Stab. YOU.

You better be good, or Tommy Mason will get you.

The children's librarian was inconsolable. Her mind wandered; her story times made no sense; she forgot the words to "The Wheels on the Bus." She also forgot to feed the rabbit, who died a week later. The cage had to be covered with cloth so the children wouldn't peep in. The rabbit lay in state all morning, till someone from the DPW could come and haul it away.

"You know," said the children's librarian to the head of

cataloging that day," she told me, 'I've had a good life. If I died tomorrow, I'd have no regrets.'" The head of cataloging stared, thinking, *That rabbit said no such thing.*

"Suzanne," said the children's librarian. "I don't care about the rabbit. I'm talking about Suzanne."

Which, when the news made its way around the library, struck us as stupid. She had children who grieved for her—isn't that regret enough? How could sunny Suzanne, sunny Juliet, with her book and her dark hair and her three beloved and loving children, think that if she had to die tomorrow, she wouldn't mind? We thought perhaps she had lost her life through carelessness and underappraisal. We wouldn't be so free with our own lives. The difference is, no one has ever wanted ours.

Did he love her? We had encyclopedias of criminals, anthologies of love poems, textbooks on abnormal psychology. All useless. The newspaper articles said that he admitted nothing, including love. "He's scared," said his lawyer. We never heard him speak, and maybe we never would.

The bitter head of reference read newspaper articles, sick that he'd ever distrusted Juliet. At night, he had dreams of Suzanne Cunningham standing on the reading-room balcony. He saw himself presenting her things, back issues of magazines, rare tax forms, the best-reviewed books. Anything to win her back.

The bunny was dead. Perhaps the children's librarian had killed it, but she claimed the rabbit was simply old, and she was the only one who knew anything about rabbits. That day with the bunny beneath its cloth, we thought we should have a funeral behind the library, out by the staff parking. We could turn it into something educational and useful, a children's program on death. Didn't parents always bury pets with a small lecture, a made-up eulogy, a somber taps played on a hand held to the mouth like a trumpet? Maybe—

"It's a fucking rabbit," said the children's librarian, in full hearing of Preschool Arts and Crafts. "It doesn't stand for anything." Then she sighed. "I'll miss Jessica," she said.

Jessica? She must have meant Juliet.

"Jessica," she said. "Jessica Rabbit."

Tommy Mason had three sisters who looked like him, all of whom seemed to be about the same age, twins or Irish twins or a combination of both. They were tall and blond and had beautiful skin with rosy, radishy cheeks, red with white beneath. They started coming back to the library with the grandfather's card. He still needed books.

For a while, they rotated duty. Then one started coming in week after week. She was a thin girl, the oldest Mason kid, someone said. Perhaps twenty years old. Pretty, like Juliet—like Suzanne—but pale, a mirror image. They could have been allegorical pictures in an old painting, or sisters on a soap opera, even though Suzanne Cunningham had been years older. Tommy Mason's sister carried the grandfather's library card and never spoke to anyone.

Somehow, we loved her. She seemed brave; she nodded when we nodded at her. We almost forgot who she was, the same way we almost forgot that Janice had ever been a nervous young man with a robot obsession and a faint, endearing mustache. She had become herself.

Ours had been a fine building until the mid-1970s, when it had the misfortune of being introduced to the wrong sort of architect. He knocked down the grand marble staircases that had led from the entrance to the reading room, and sealed off the first floor from the upstairs; he installed coarse brick walls and staircases that were only staircases, only transportation. It was possible for the people who worked in the first-floor departments—children's, circulation—to go days without seeing their upstairs colleagues.

So the day the children's librarian went up to reference and ran into Tommy Mason's sister might have been the first day the two had met at all. Circulation knew the Mason girl well; reference saw her as she deliberated among the mysteries. The children's librarian rarely left her room, its puppets, its jigsaw puzzles. Somebody else had taken over feeding the finches and the fish.

She recognized Tommy Mason's sister from news reports or neighborhood gossip. She stared for a while, confirmed the identity with the head of reference. No harm in answering, he thought.

Tommy Mason's sister was in the mysteries, because that's what her grandfather still read. Maybe he needed to read them especially now, to know that murders happened in this way: someone was killed, and there were clues and an explanation, and at the very end a madman or bitter wife was led away, and nobody but the murderer wept. She looked at the books, at the skull-and-crossbones stickers the cataloging department stuck on the spines of mysteries.

She selected three and tucked them close to her chest and was halfway across the floor to the stairs when the children's librarian stepped in front of her and said, "I knew her, you know."

Tommy Mason's sister looked towards the ground. That was where she always looked. The children's librarian tried to lower herself into eyeshot.

"I knew the woman your brother murdered." And then, in her storytelling voice, the calm one that explained that Rosetta Stone was a thing and not a person and wasn't that wonderful, she said, "Your brother's a monster. A freak."

Everyone watched the two of them, the children's librarian with her tough, tiny soldier's shoes, Tommy Mason's sister dressed the way all the library teenagers dressed: baggy pants, sneakers, a hooded warm-up jacket—ready, the way they all were, for an escape. Except she didn't. She stood there, and then she turned away and walked to a table. The children's librarian went downstairs. She gave her footsteps extra echo. Tommy Mason's sister sat and began to cry.

It didn't look serious at first, and people tried to give her privacy. She held the books to her as if they were a compress for her heart, and tears slid down her face and onto the table, which was itself carved with hearts, declarations of love and being: CK WAS HERE. WANDA + BILLY. We didn't know anything about her. We didn't even know her first name.

She stayed there for an hour. The reference librarians didn't know what to do. One of them approached her, said, "Dear, can I call somebody?" The girl didn't move. Her

tears were so regular they seemed mechanical, manufac-
tured inside her for this purpose: to darken the wooden
table in front of her, to pave the carved grooves of graffiti.

The head of reference called down to the children's
room. "I don't care," he said into the phone. "You come up
here." The other librarians thought that this was like asking the snake that bit you to come suck out the venom.

You could tell the children's librarian expected to be
chewed out. She figured that the girl she'd accused was long
gone, that her matter-of-fact words were just one more
thing that the Masons would discuss, outraged, over dinner. But there the girl was.

So, then. The children's librarian sat at the table. Such a
clumsy young woman, really. She whispered something to
the crying girl. She reached to touch the girl's elbow. The
elbow stayed put.

I didn't, said the children's librarian.

No response.

I'm lost—

—for words,—without her.

A dead person is lost property. You know this. Still,
you've been searching for what was taken. You know—
you've been schooled in this fact—that what you owned
will never be returned to you. But you're still owed something. You can't eat lunch with your friend, her fingers
marking chess moves across the board. You can't hear those
same fingers on a computer keyboard or feel them on your
shoulder at a time you need them. People take their hands
with them, no matter where they go.

Surely there is happiness somewhere in the world. And

God will forgive you if, for a moment, you labor under the common misconception that happiness is created—you'd swear one of the students has done a science-fair project on this—when two unhappy people collide and one of them makes the other unhappier. It's steam, it's energy. It works: you feel something rise in you. But it doesn't last.

The children's librarian began to cry, too. Not like Tommy Mason's sister, beautiful in her sorrow, but like one of the toddlers refused longer visiting hours with the bunny. She rearranged her features into something terrible. When she caught her breath, you could hear it, you would think it hurt. Nobody felt sorry for her. Then she left the table and walked up the stairs to the balcony to watch what would happen. As she passed the reference desk, she said, "Call her family."

They had to find the phone number by looking up Tommy Mason's library record. His card was still delinquent.

"Is this Mr. Mason?" the head of reference asked. That sounded frightening. He tried, "Your daughter—" but that was worse. Then he said, "This is the library—" as if the building were calling. "This is the library, Mr. Mason. Your daughter is fine, she's here, but I think you better pick her up."

The entire family arrived, and the father with his florid face sat next to her at the table. *Sarah*, he said, *don't you want to go home? Let's go home, Sarah,* and then the mother and sisters said it, too: *Let's go home, Sarah.* They stayed there awhile, and we wondered whether they'd ever leave.

Maybe they'd move in. There were worse places for a trou-
bled family to live. We had plenty of books and magazines.
We had a candy machine downstairs. They could move into
the religion section in the corner, a quiet, untouched neighborhood with a window. They could string up a curtain
and never be bothered. A nice cul-de-sac far from the chaos
of the cookbooks, the SAT guides.

They did not look up to see the children's librarian on
the dull staircase. Sarah did not direct them there.

The Masons bundled Sarah up in their eight bare arms,
the devoted family octopus, and led her out the door. She
was a child who could be rescued. She could be taken home
and given a meal and put to bed; they could slip the puffy
sneakers she wore off her feet. In the morning, the sneakers
would still be there where she'd left them, waiting for her to
put them on and pull the laces tight and live the rest of her
life.

The books in her arms set the alarm off on the way out.
No one stopped her.

Up on the balcony stairs, the children's librarian stopped
crying. She didn't move. The few patrons there stepped
around her, because there was only the one staircase. The
head of reference went to her. He sat down; he set his hand
on her shoulder to steady himself.

"You've done a terrible thing," he said, and she nodded.
Then he took her hand, the way he wished he had taken
Juliet's hand, or Sarah's—or a dozen sad girls he'd known
before but never discussed. "Everyone does," he said.

"Not everyone," said the children's librarian.

"You just know that you have, that's all."

The Masons would have been home by then. We thought we could feel the door of the house, closing behind them.

It's been months since Sarah left us, more months since Juliet died. The Masons gave up and moved to another city nearby; Tommy Mason hasn't even gone on trial yet, though they've decided that when he does, it will be as a juvenile and not as an adult. He's in the news every now and then. The family goes to another library, in a town where the grandfather was never a mayor and Mason is an unremarkable name and their blond looks don't mean anything. But they don't know that their library is in our computer network. Their new library is a relative of ours, which means we can look their cards up on the computer if we want to, we can renew their books and erase their fines and wonder if they ever think about us.

The children's librarian is living with her cruel thing. We have forgiven her. We go into the children's room. She is silent behind the desk cutting out Santa Clauses or Easter eggs or autumn leaves, which children will cover with cotton balls and glitter. We talk to the finches, those filthy creatures. We imagine opening the cage and telling them to go ahead—it wouldn't be the first time—they should go ahead and fly. Even though we don't open the door, we tell them anyhow. Stranger things, we tell them, have happened.

The House of Two
Three-Legged Dogs

In the December rain, the buildings around the town square were the color of dirty fingernails. Still, the French had tried to jolly things up a bit. Decorations hung from streetlamps, though at midday, Tony couldn't tell what lit bulbs would reveal at night: A curried prawn? A goiter? People had dangled toddler-size nylon Father Christmases out their windows, each with a shoulder-borne sack of presents. There were dozens of Father Christmases, and they hung slack, sodden, like snagged kites. They looked lynched.

Tony drove the rattletrap Escort he'd just bought around Bazaillac's covered market a second time. He and Izzy and the kids had lived in the countryside nearby for eleven years. At the start, people in town called them *Les Anglais*, because they were the only ones. Now the whole valley was overrun with English. You could fly into Bergerac for three quid on Ryanair, flash the mere cover of your passport to the on-duty Frenchman, and strike out. You could buy an old presbytery or millhouse for next to nothing, turn the outbuildings into *gîtes* and rent them for the summer, and then sit back and live the good life—or so the English thought. They renovated or half-renovated the properties and then lost interest, complained about how many other English were in the area: you couldn't go into a market without being assaulted by the terrible voices of your countrymen. Tony had heard that Slovenia and Macedonia were the new places to go. He wished Slovenia and Macedonia luck.

In the meantime he was looking for his son. The car was a present for him, and Tony was now struck by a problem: he wanted to hand Malcolm the keys and walk away, but Malcolm, if he were found, would be drunk, wanting to keep drinking, and then how would Tony get home?

They'd figure it out, he decided.

Sunday, winter: nothing was open but Bar le Tip Top on one side of the square, and the Café du Commerce on the opposite. Both were pretty much Anglophone bars now. The frivolous drinkers might start out in the Tip Top and then cross under the covered market to the Commerce for a change of scenery. The serious drinkers stayed put at the Commerce. Tony's son, Malcolm, was a serious drinker.

Between the rain on the outside and the smoke and condensation on the inside, the Commerce window was a blur of fairy lights and whitewashed lunch specials. The arcade was deep, and in good weather, Emile, the owner, set up tables under the arches; now there was only a creaking sign-board listing the day's menu. Tony stared at the door and tried to will Malcolm through it, but Malcolm had never once stopped drinking because of Tony's will or wishes or pleas or even—embarrassingly, Tony hated to remember it—tears. He looked back across the square. A fat man ambled underneath the market roof: Sid, another serious drinker, whom Tony knew from his own days of serious drinking. Tony honked. Sid turned, his gray beard tinseled with wet, his bald head cloud-colored in the market's shadows. In his peach sweatpants and jacket he looked like the washing-up cloth of the gods, soaked and proud. The Escort's window required three hands to open, so Tony cracked the door instead. Sid pulled it open.

"Good God," said Sid. He leaned his head into the car. "Where'd the car come from? Bloody *Knight Rider*."

"What?" said Tony.

"*Knight Rider*. You've seen that program. Talking car? Hasselhoff?"

"No idea," said Tony. "Have you seen Malcolm? The car's for him. Christmas present." He'd bought it from a fleeing Italian. He didn't know whether a car would make a difference, but he hoped so.

"Reminds me," said Sid. "Where are you off to? The house? I have something for you."

Someone shouted from the door of the Commerce. Not Malcolm. The Maori ex-footballer stepped out, smiling expansively. His English girlfriend—someone else's wife—hooked her chin on his shoulder and stared in desolation.

She had money. The Maori was a kept man. Together they looked like the masks of comedy and tragedy on a proscenium arch.

Sid stood up and his stomach, an impressive spherical object, came into the car, crowding Tony over. "*Knight Rider,* hey?" he called across. He pounded on the roof of the car.

"HahahahahaHA!" said the Maori, nodding in his disconcerting, rapid-fire way. "Sid! Absolutely! You drinking, Sidney?"

Sid leaned back into the car. These days he was mostly Malcolm's friend, though he was Tony's age. He had the unsavory charisma of a man on a remote island who'd let himself be worshipped by the natives as a god, who might even use his watch and pocket torch as signs of his divinity. "You going home, yeah?" he said to Tony. "I have something to bring you. Be over in a tick. One jar and I'm there. All right?"

"Have you seen Malcolm?" Tony repeated.

"No, mate," said Sid. "Not for a few days."

"Ask the Maori, is he in the bar?"

"Christ, you think he's a Maori? He's a sham. He only *claims*—"

"Ask him."

Sid sighed and straightened up, and the stomach reasserted itself. "Colin?" he called across the car. "Malcolm back?"

The Maori laughed and shook his head.

"Sorry, mate," Sid told Tony, slapping the top of the car again. "See you in a bit."

Tony watched him cross over. Beneath the arcade, the Maori tried to *faire la bise,* but Sid did not submit to kisses; Sid ducked. They went inside. All the various Irish Johns would be there, too. There were so many now, according to Malcolm, they had to number them: John the Irish One, John the Irish Two, and so on. They were up to John the Irish Eight.

In the wintertime the Commerce was filled with the skint and the rowdy. Any one of the regulars could be accused of drinking himself to death, but all together and out in public and in France, they were merely living the good life. Who wouldn't rather drink himself to death in a foreign country? Your mother couldn't nag you, the wine was cheap. You weren't in danger of drinking yourself to mere ruined health.

The Commerce had been his and Izzy's local when they could still afford bars, back before the bankruptcy. They went every night under the pretense of improving their French. It was a long, dark, friendly bar, with a snooker table in the middle and a vending machine that dispensed cans of nuts at the front. The girls and Malcolm loved that machine; they were practically brought up at its foot. They'd turn the big cold key that worked the mechanism and check for fallen coins or cans of peanuts, even though Emile put out baskets of peanuts for free.

Malcolm had been ten years old when he'd come to France. He'd been living with his mother and stepfather, and one night the stepfather had called up Tony. "He's hard to get along with, this kid. Don't you think?" No, Tony didn't think. If Malcolm had a fault, it was that he got along too well, with angels and sinners: his teachers cried when they had to punish him. At any rate he was put on the ferry, and Tony had met him, and brought him to the house to live with him and his stepmother and stepsisters, and together they went nightly to a bar, where the boy learned to speak French and to drink hard without ever taking a lesson in either. At that front table he turned from a cowering child into a charming sot.

It's a shame about us, Tony thought. It was a shame, for instance, that he and Izzy had exactly the same weaknesses and bad habits. They were both terrible with money, and they had a soft spot for animals. No, soft spot didn't cover it. They were about animals the way some of their friends were about drink: They snuck abandoned animals into the house. They bought animals with money they didn't have. They swore they needed no more animals in the morning and showed up with more animals in the evening. They had two three-legged dogs, two four-legged dogs, several puppies, six indoor cats, countless outdoor cats, untold kittens, goats, the old horse Nelson, at least fifty budgies. They would be ruined by animals.

But when the farmer down the road appears at your house with a three-legged dog and explains that he knows you already have one—apparently a single three-legged dog is all you need to become famous for three-legged dogs—what can you do? And if your two three-legged dogs fall in love, and your new three-legged dog ends up pregnant by your old three-legged dog—well, you'd have to have a harder heart than Tony had to send all those four-legged puppies away.

He hid the Escort in the barn because he hadn't told Izzy about it: they'd decided not to exchange presents this year. The house was cold inside, a shambles. They'd bought it two years before from a Dutchman who had run it briefly as a home for delinquent French boys. Then the boys ran away, or were taken away by the government, leaving behind eight bedrooms smelling of piss and three outbuildings that had been set mildly on fire. Tony and Izzy bought the property for nothing, practically, though even that "nothing" was a gift from Tony's father. "Buy this house outright," he'd said. "I'm tired of worrying about you." The bankruptcy laws in France were awful: for years they would not be allowed to own property, to even have a bank account. The French would teach them a lesson. So they'd had to put the house in Malcolm's name; the girls were underage at the time. They'd hoped he'd rise to the occasion.

At the far end of the main room, the kitchen lay in pieces. A bag of garbage sat on the sofa like a person. Tony moved it, then filled a carafe of wine from the box on the kitchen island and set it on the mantelpiece to warm. He built a fire in the stove underneath. Izzy would be with the budgies. He decided to leave her alone.

"Hello, little mother," he said to Macy, who lay in her basket nursing her pitch-black pups. She was a poodle the way Malcolm and the girls were French: generally she could pass, but an authentic poodle might find her a little vulgar. Now she lifted her head and regarded Tony with the weary love of a woman for a dissolute husband. There was a knock at the door. She looked at it.

"I'll get it," Tony told her.

The puppies took no notice, and the four-legged dogs were elsewhere, but Aldo came skittering down the hall in full bark and filled the room with hysterics that woke up all but the most blasé of the kittens. His missing front leg and barrel-chested Airedale's bark gave him a wounded-veteran air.

"Aldo!" Tony told him, trying to hook his leg around the dog's prow as he opened the door. "Back. *Back*."

Sid seemed to have swollen in the rain. "Oh, bark bark bark," he said, wiping his feet theatrically. Under his arm was a bell-shaped birdcage, and inside the birdcage was a gray parrot with a red tail.

"Voilà," he said. "Christmas present from your only be-gotten son."

"A parrot," said Tony.

"Well spotted," said Sid. "A parrot indeed."

The parrot clutched the bars of the cage in its beak. Its black eyes were set in rings of white feathers. It opened its beak delicately and showed a black tongue, then casually flapped its wings. In his rib cage Tony felt a similar cautious flapping. So his heart still worked. *"Je m'appelle Clothilde,"* the parrot said. Her accent was terrible.

"Hello, beauty," Tony said to her. "Oh, hello, darling. This is from Malcolm? Isn't she lovely? Aldo. Aldo, down. Shush. For God's sake."

"That'll be fifty euro," Sid said. "Here, take 'er. D'ye mind? Wet out here. May I?"

"For what?" said Tony.

"What for what?"

"Fifty euro for what?"

"For the bird." Sid shouldered a path into the room and bobbed his head in an avian way, as though it were his only means of seeing in three dimensions. He yawned, doglike; his tongue was black, too, stained with red wine. Aldo sniffed the back of his knee, barked once, then noticed the fire and curled up by the stove.

"I thought it was a—"

"Fifty down, fifty on delivery. D'ye mind?" He'd already hooked his elbow at the bottom of his filthy fleece top and was flipping it up. "Just till I dry."

Before France, Sid had been a visiting lecturer in drama at an American university and must have owned actual clothing, with zippers and buttons and DRY CLEAN ONLY tags, but Tony had never seen him in anything other than exercise togs for the very fat. Sid tossed the fleece top on the back of the sofa and began to thoughtfully palm his bare stomach. From the hip bones down—the part of Sid in perpetual darkness, the territory in the shadow of his belly—he seemed to be a slender man. But his stomach was extraordinary: round and high and tight and gravity-defying. He showed it to the cast-iron stove, ostensibly for purposes of evaporation, though it looked to Tony like more of a challenge: *Get a load of me,* stomach seemed to say to fire.

"I forget," he said, looking at the half-smashed walls. "How long have you been in this house?"

"This one? Two years," said Tony, embarrassed. "We've been in France—"

Sid gave a low whistle. "You got your work cut out for you, son."

"Work takes money."

"How many bedrooms?"

"Too many. Eight."

Sid swung back and forth with his hands on his stomach. He seemed to be dowsing for something. "How much the Dutchman ask for it?"

"Can't remember. Not much."

"It's fucking raining," Sid said.

"Has been," said Tony. "This bird. Is she really a present from Malcolm?"

"Happy Crimbo," Sid said.

"He gave you fifty euro?"

Sid nodded absentmindedly and eyed the wine. "A hundred euro is a terrific price for an African gray. They'll run eight hundred in a store."

"Sure," said Tony. The bird squawked and paced her cage, and Tony again felt his heart mimic back. He had no intention of paying Sid. "I used to have a gray like this."

"What happened?"

"She died."

"As they will," said Sid. "When?"

"When I was twelve. My father gave her to me. I loved that bird for a while."

"What happened?"

"Oh," said Tony. "My father taught her to talk. Religious things. Said the bird found religion. *Repent your sins. Baby Jesus. What a friend we have in Jesus.*"

"Nothing less tolerable than a godly bird," said Sid.

"She was ill after she got religious. Then she died. My father told me they usually lived for decades and decades, parrots. I don't think I ever got over it."

He'd told that story to Malcolm, and Malcolm had remembered. Clothilde. A lady African gray. The females were always crankier, he recalled, and she bit at the cage again. He set her on the ground.

"Now then. A drink?"

Sid turned and smiled. "What are you offering?"

"Pineau, beer. I could make you a gin, wine—"

"Pineau!" said Sid. "It's *such* a nice drink. The angels weep. But it's not pineau weather, is it? Is that wine there? Is that wine for *me*?"

"Let me get glasses," said Tony. The cupboards were on the floor, waiting to be hung. The four-legged dogs came careening down the main stairs and into the room, herding an adolescent kitten.

"Sheepdogs?" Sid asked.

"Of some stripe, maybe." Louis and Borgia certainly had the gap-mouthed, hunch-shouldered look of sheepdogs, but Tony suspected an actual sheep would scare the crap out of them. Mostly they bumped into things and tried to look as though they meant to do it. Borgia sometimes tried to herd the kitchen island; a kitten was an improvement. Now she saw the parrot and began to herd that.

"That bird's not going anywhere," said Tony, taking the carafe from the mantelpiece. "That bird is caged."

Borgia stopped, her head at an obsequious tilt.

"Right," said Tony to the bird. He lifted her cage and put her on the coffee table. Sid collapsed into the old leather armchair.

"*Je t'aime, Olivier,*" said Clothilde, and Tony thought: *Nothing sounds more insincere than a parrot speaking French.*

The wine tasted like buttered popcorn. Sid lit a cigarette. "D'ye mind?" he said again, as though it were polite to ask even if he disregarded the answer.

"Izzy's asthma," said Tony, helplessly.

"Izzy's not here."

"She's—"

"She's not in the room," clarified Sid. "Where is she?"

"Budgies," said Tony.

"What?"

"She's in the budgie room."

That was the advantage and danger of an eight-bedroom house: eventually the oddest things would have their own rooms. When Malcolm sold the house—if Malcolm sold the house—the new owners would walk around sniffing, saying, as Tony and Izzy had before them, "What do you suppose they did in *this* room?"

"Ah, the budgies," said Sid. "I've never met the budgies. Did you know that *budgerigar* means 'good eating' in the Aboriginal language?"

"I hope it doesn't come to that," said Tony.

"That would make you a psittiphage," said Sid.

"A what?"

"A psittiphage: an eater of parrots. Psittiphobe: one who fears parrots. Psittophile: one who—"

"Yes," said Tony. He filled Sid's glass again.

"So you already have parrots, and now here's another."

"The budgies are Izzy's minions. This one's mine. I don't even like those budgies. I love you, though," he said to Clothilde. "Do you love me?"

She bobbed her head and said nothing.

"They talk?"

"The budgies? One or two," said Tony. Most of them couldn't, they just babbled. Then suddenly one would say *Hello, there. Hello, there.* It always made Tony feel as though he'd been doing something vile in a room full of deaf and dumb and blind nuns, only to find there were a few regular nuns mixed in.

"Anthony," Sid said grimly.

"What?"

Sid pointed at him. He waved his finger around, indicating something in general about Tony that was displeasing him. "Your hair," he said at last. "Your beard. It's a disgrace."

"I need a trim."

"One or the other. No man should ever keep his beard and hair the same length. Shave your head and let your beard go, or grow your hair and affect a Vandyke. One or the other. As it is, you just look *fuzzy*."

"I *am* fuzzy," said Tony. He rubbed his hair ostentatiously and stared at Sid's bald head.

"All right," said Sid. "I get your point."

"I am fuzzy," Tony said sadly.

"I know, mate."

"Malcolm tell you?"

"Malcolm tell me what?"

But Tony couldn't say it aloud.

Sid lumbered to his feet and snagged the carafe off the mantelpiece. He poured himself another glass. *"Jamais deux sans trois,"* he said, *Never two without three,* the drinker's motto. He took a great gulp, then looked at Tony. "Bloody rude of me!" he said, filled Tony's glass, too, and splashed the rest of the wine into his own. He held the empty carafe by the neck and pointed to the corner.

"What's wrong with that dog?" Sid took a drink.

"That's Macy," said Tony.

"But what's wrong with her?" Sid took another drink.

"That's *Macy*."

"But what happened to her?" Another drink.

After a second, Tony said, "Land mine."

"That's not what I mean. She's all, she's got, she's *swollen*." Sid indicated his own bare torso with the empty carafe and finished the wine. It was just like Sid to be prudish about a dog's teats.

"She's nursing. She had pups. You want one?"

"I live in a truck," said Sid. He held out both the wine glass and the carafe.

Tony went to the box of wine on the kitchen island. "Don't look," he said, filling the carafe.

"*I* don't care."

"I was talking to Clothilde."

"I don't mean to harp on the fifty euro," said Sid, "but it is fifty euro."

"Yeah, yeah," said Tony. "Where'd Malcolm find her?"

"Mine."

"Yours?"

He looked at the parrot with some suspicion and came back to fill Sid's wine glass. Sid watched the rising level with the concentration of a telekinetic.

"You're selling her why?"

"I see we'll be ordering off the children's menu," said Sid, and then, with cruel patience, "I *live*. In. A. *Truck*."

"Kids don't want it?"

"*She* won't," said Sid. He shook his head. He'd been sitting like a human being. Now he wheeled around in the chair and draped his legs over one arm and leaned on the other. Some wine slopped and he sucked it off the back of his hand. The armchair seemed to falter with its burden. "Spent the morning tearing down the piggery," he said.

"You have a piggery?"

"Had a piggery. Hated the piggery. The piggery is no more."

"I thought you lived in a truck."

"There's this house," said Sid. "Nearby Manville, this side of the river."

"When did you buy that?"

"Haven't yet. Will do. The *mairie*'s deciding whether it's habitable. I'm getting a jump on the work. Night, mostly."

"What if they decide it isn't?"

"They will."

"You're renovating a house you don't own in secret—"

Sid sighed dramatically. "I am," he declared, "over France. Isn't that what they say? I am so *over* France."

"Leave," said Tony. He moved to the sofa.

"My kids are here," said Sid. "I might drink a pineau."

He looked a bit cross-eyed, Tony thought, but maybe it was Tony who was drunk.

Apparently all American university lecturers slept with their students, but Sid, bored by the timorous bad behavior of the Yanks, who knew how to fuck up only a semester—a real man took pains to fuck up his *life*—had carried one off to Las Vegas and married her. That was how he'd lost his job. "Should have waited till final grades were in," he'd once told Tony. "That, or not married her at all." They'd moved to France with plans to open an English-language theater near Eymet. Tony had no notion when they'd given up on the idea. Now they had two little kids, a son and a daughter, and Sid made his living as a chippie's assistant: he toted wood for a friend who was a master carpenter.

"Perhaps I'll take that pineau," Sid prodded.

So Tony got the pineau. It was sweet and thick and cold, and he and Sid drank it in big gulps, though it was meant to be an apéritif.

"The angels weep," said Sid.

"I don't know who gave us this bottle," said Tony, looking at the label.

"Bonjour," said the bird.

Sid fought to sit up. His stomach seemed to be the sun around which the rest of his body orbited. "Pay her off and she'll love you forever. Isn't that how it works in the slave-girl movies? Tony," he said, "I hate to hound you, but—I'd ask Malcolm—"

"I don't have it."

"Izzy have it?"

"Izzy has the same no-money I have."

"The budgie room," said Sid dreamily. "That sounds nice. Let's go see the budgie room and talk to Izzy."

"We're not going to the budgie room."

"I like budgies," said Sid, hurt.

"I don't."

But Sid was already struggling to his feet.

"*Je t'aime*," said the bird again, and Sid said, "Kid, you're breaking my heart."

Tony followed Sid, and Aldo followed Tony, and Macy, yawning, followed Aldo. They walked down the hallway Indian file. From behind, Sid had the tight-arsed bullish strut of a smuggler. His bare back looked strong; he hitched up his sweatpants with one hand and almost kicked a passing kitten down the hallway. "You seem to be infested with kittens," he observed. "Hello, you," he said to it, leaning down and plucking it from under Aldo's snuffling nose. It was one of the little kittens. Tony could hear its ingratiating purr. It was true: they were infested with kittens.

"You want a kitten?" he asked.

"I *still* live in a truck," said Sid. In a kingly fashion, he handed Tony his empty wine glass, as though it were a decree he wanted enacted instantly. He held on to the kitten.

"Izzy might be asleep," said Tony.

"Oh, she'll see *me*."

Sid had epaulets of steel-gray hair on his shoulders. The

kitten, high on the curve of his stomach, looked dwarfish and blissful. You kind of had to love the pair of them.

"I'll get you a drink," said Tony. "Second door on your left."

In the kitchen Tony tossed the empty pineau bottle and re-filled the carafe. *Jamais deux sans trois*. The spigot was hard to work, and the wine was running out, so he opened the cardboard box and extracted the metallic bladder and squeezed it like an udder into the carafe, from which he then filled Sid's glass. If he'd been sober, he thought, he would never have let Sid bother Izzy; and he was very happy he wasn't sober, because it was essential that *someone* bother Izzy. Aldo had followed him back and now sniffed one of the puppies skeptically. "He does so look like you," Tony told him.

When he opened the door to the budgie room one of the budgies flew out, a yellow lutino. That left forty-nine inside.

Sid and Izzy were sitting on the awful flowered sofa holding hands; it was the room's only piece of furniture meant for humans. The sprung-open cages of the budgies encircled them. Some budgies—the ones who feared the warden, no doubt—stayed in their cages, but most of them flew around like drunken fairies. The grouch-faced English budgie called Bomber Harris paced pacifically through Izzy's spiky blond hair. The way Izzy and Sid sat—he still bare-chested, holding a sleeping kitten in one hand near his armpit, she with her birds—they looked like a low-budget allegorical painting, though what the allegory was, Tony couldn't say. Izzy was a bird-inclined saint who attracted budgies with her kindness, or a crazy woman who stuffed her pockets with bread crumbs. If she'd been ten years younger and twenty pounds thinner, it would have been saint for sure.

"Should that cat be in here, with all these birds?" Tony asked.

"It's fine," said Sid. "I have her hypnotized."

"Malcolm bought me a parrot," Tony said to Izzy.

"*Malcolm* did?"

"Half a parrot," said Sid, patting the back of her hand. Then he hissed at Tony, "When did this *happen*?"

"Oh, *hello*," said Bomber Harris in a ludicrously pleasant voice. "Oh, *hello*."

"Week ago," said Tony. "An African gray. Like Maud." He began to drink the glass of wine he'd brought for Sid.

Izzy rolled her eyes at Maud's name. "If you met that bird today, you'd never give her a second look."

"Attention," said Sid. "This did not happen in a week."

"The budgies?" Izzy scooped Bomber Harris off her head and smiled at him. "They tell you that if you want to breed budgies you can't have a pair, a pair won't mate. You need at least two pair. So we got four pair to make sure. Eventually—"

"Because they're swingers," asked Sid, "or because they're naive? Should the other pair be older and come with sex manuals or be younger and come with quaaludes?"

"*Quaaludes?*" said Izzy. "Do quaaludes even exist anymore?"

"Since Malcolm," said Tony.

"Since Malcolm *what?*" said Sid.

Since Malcolm had made his announcement—*I'm selling the house*—she'd slept in the budgie room on the old, moldy flowered sofa they'd found in the barn. At night she draped the cages, then blacked out her own head with a duvet. *I've talked to a lawyer. It's in my name.* The budgie room had belonged to the worst of the badly behaved French boys, the one who seemed to have pissed in every corner of the room though the toilet was right there, the one who carved his name, PASQUAL, in the stone walls, and put his cigarettes out on the windowsill, and broke the lock on the window so he could creep out at night; by all evidence a feral boy—the budgies kept finding long dark hairs—but nevertheless a boy who most likely had never threatened to sell his parents' house from under them. *I'm sorry to do it.* When had Malcolm become so tall? His hair was cut like the guitar players of Tony's 1970s youth, shaggy, awful even then. *It's just when I look at my problems, I don't see any other way.* Izzy loved Malcolm, though she wasn't his mother, and was taking his betrayal worse than Tony—which is to say, she believed it would actually happen. *All right? Dad? Daddy?* Everyone loved Malcolm. Sometimes Tony thought that was Malcolm's problem, overexposure to the rays of love, a kind of melanoma of the soul.

I don't have a choice, said Malcolm, and Izzy said, *Of course you do, you make the choice to be a better person.*

But Tony understood, then and now. There was a small part of him that believed he'd sell out every single person he loved, too, if it allowed him to be rid of his obligations of love forever.

He stared at the brown drapes Izzy kept drawn so the budgies wouldn't fly into the window. That couldn't be healthy, surely. Even a bird needed vitamin D. He couldn't explain to Sid what Malcolm planned to do. He refused to believe in it. To believe in it was to yank at the one loose thread that would eventually, finally, unravel their entire lives. It was hot in the room, and Tony imagined a house-hunter asking about the heat. *Gas? Oil? Wood?*

No, actually: budgies.

Tony hoped. Izzy didn't, and she was the one who explained it all to Sid.

When she'd finished, Sid began to sink. He sank as though the vital architecture of his skeleton were being dismantled, as though, in a moment, like a tent the gossamer bulk of him would billow to the ground. *Shit,* Tony thought. *If Sid is appalled, it's serious.*

"No," Sid said. "Malcolm? No."

"Malcolm," said Izzy. "That beautiful kid."

"When?"

She laughed. "He says the place needs to be fixed up first, so."

Sid got up. He pointed the kitten at Tony like a gun. "You need a lawyer. Someone French, who knows those laws, because they're set up to fuck you every way they can. They will *betray you*!" The kitten curled its sleeping body around Sid's hand. "Izzy, listen to me. Do you know a lawyer?"

Izzy shrugged her entire body infinitesimally, to illustrate the impossibility of this.

"Money," said Sid, nodding. "I know a bloke looking for a car." He turned to Tony. "All right, Knight Rider. You're selling the Ford."

"What Ford?" said Izzy.

Tony shook his head.

"You say it's for Malcolm. For *Malcolm*," said Sid, disgusted. "I say, sell *all* his Christmas presents."

"That's the only one," said Tony.

Izzy rubbed her head and her hair bristled. He hated that haircut. "You bought him a car?"

"A crap car," said Tony. "Twenty-five euro." Actually it had been a hundred. The Italian had been desperate.

"Malcolm is in England," said Sid; and Izzy repeated, in a wondering sorrowful voice, "Malcolm is in England?"

"What's Malcolm doing in *England*?" Tony asked.

Sid sat back down on the sofa. "You didn't know Malcolm was in England?"

"What's he *doing* there?" said Tony.

"I don't know. But he's gone. Christmas with his mother? Said he was going, hasn't been at the Commerce, and if Malcolm hasn't been at the Commerce then he's not in the country. I know someone looking for a car. This Englishman who married an American. The fool. How much do you want for it? They have a budget. It's not much. Three hundred euro."

"It's not worth—"

"Sell it," said Izzy. "If that's their budget, that's what it's worth."

Three hundred euro seemed simultaneously an enormous sum of money and so little it wasn't even worth thinking about.

"It's Malcolm's," said Tony again.

"*Who cares!*" Sid pulled a cell phone from his pocket, looked at the screen, and shook it.

"No reception," said Izzy. "End of the driveway."

"Fuck it. I'll go get them. They're staying with Little Aussie Peter. Back in a tick. I'll try to talk them up. All right, Tony? Pay attention. Action stations. The car runs?" He stood up and suddenly noticed he was still holding a kitten. "Hello, moggy. Let's go. The car?"

"Those old diesels run forever."

"That's all they need. Cash in hand, I'll tell them. Bye, Izzy darling."

"Bye, Sidney," she said. "Take that parrot with you."

"She's my parrot," said Tony. "Her name's Clothilde."

"*Clothilde!*" said Izzy, as though the name itself were an argument against the bird.

This was finally how their marriage would drift apart: Tony didn't understand loving fifty birds at a time, and Izzy didn't understand loving only one. Tony followed Sid down the hallway. "He might change his mind."

"He won't change his mind. What have you done with my clothing?" Sid asked the kitten, who meowed in an incensed, kittenish way. "Ah, here."

In the front room, Clothilde knocked her beak on her cage and said, "Aye-aye-aye." Somehow Sid managed to pull on the fleece top while still holding the kitten, though his head spent some time investigating first one armhole and then the other before at last finding the neck. "When was its last *contrôle technique?*"

"Not too long ago."

"Aye, aye," said Clothilde.

"More than six months? Because otherwise you'll have to do it again, and will it pass?"

"Aye!" Clothilde said.

"It'll pass," said Tony, who hadn't checked the date. "Listen. He's not that bad. When it comes down to doing the worst thing—"

Sid had his hand on the door. He smelled sweet and winey, and his eyes looked like the back end of a globe, some place where the Earth was mostly oceans and unpronounceable islands, some place to fear cannibals. *Please,* Tony thought, *don't tell me you know him better than I do.*

"The worst thing is saying," said Sid.

"What?"

"The worst thing is he told you he *would.* He's done the worst thing. Now he's got that out of the way he can do anything. Believe me. I know." Sid handed the kitten over and opened the door. "I'll be right back. Anthony. Listen to me. It's not too late. You have to decide what kind of man you want to be."

Clothilde said, "I *love* you!" as though she'd been teaching herself in their absence, an orphan hoping to ingratiate herself to foster parents.

"I love you, too, my darling," Sid said, and closed the door behind him.

. . .

For a parrot, Clothilde seemed to have a poor sense of balance: she squawked and dug into Tony's shoulder. It had stopped raining. The outdoor cats were edging out of the old barn and sniffing the wet air. Clothilde squawked again. "You're a pretty girl," said Tony, though even he could hear the lie in his voice. She ran her beak through his hair. He kicked the cats from the barn so they wouldn't bother her, and closed the door.

In the dim light the Escort looked seaworthy. It was black, with tinted windows, and on both sides the word LASER was painted in space-age lettering. It was an '84, Malcolm's birth year, and that had seemed like a sign. Malcolm took his bike to the Commerce, and came back wobbling drunk or not at all. Sometimes he slept in a ditch—an actual ditch. "It's France, Daddy," he said. "It's not like a ditch somewhere else."

Tony had assumed Malcolm had been sleeping on sofas since he'd made his announcement, ashamed of himself. But he was in England.

He lifted the passenger door handle, remembered it opened only from the inside, and went around. The paperwork was still in the glove box. The *carte grise*—the title— was in order, and the last *contrôle technique* had been, miraculously, five months and three weeks before. He could legally sell the car to the Americans without putting it through another inspection, just as the Italian had sold it to him. That was the reason the Italian hadn't haggled, or held out for another offer.

"Bah di donc!" said the parrot.

His shoulder hurt. "All right, Clothilde," he said, and set her on the passenger seat so he could get to work.

For three hundred euro, could you expect a radio? He pulled it out, and then the safety kit: the reflective vest, the reflective triangle, the flares, all the things he'd bought for Malcolm to keep him safe and entertained. The old fuel pump had gone out and he'd replaced it with a rubber bulb: he had to open the bonnet and pump the fuel into the engine by hand, but it worked all right and a new pump would cost a hundred euro. If the Americans wanted to replace it, let them. Now he opened and pumped and slammed.

The car started. The fuel tank was full up. He got the tubing and another rubber bulb to siphon it out. He knew this was not quite decent, but the lawnmower ran on diesel, too, and fuel was expensive. He'd give the Americans directions to the Leclerc station.

"Hello," he said to Clothilde.

She gave a half whistle.

"Tell me a story," he said to her. She chewed at the edge of the seat. "Tell me the story of your life. Tell me—tell me you love me."

The dashboard looked sad with the radio gone. The steering wheel had been put on crooked at some point, which made it difficult to read the speedometer, which reminded him that the dashboard light had gone out. They could get a bulb at the Leclerc, too.

The engine stunk of oil once it heated up.

The hatchback didn't stay open. You needed a plank.

"The plank's gratis," Tony said aloud. "No charge whatsoever for the plank."

The love of a young couple for a bad car took time: you had to drive it as it grew more eccentric, as each component failed or flickered or worsened. Tony had bought the car dazzled by the price, and then added each new oddity to the story he was telling himself: Malcolm's First Car. They were going to tell that story forever. But that's not how it worked, was it.

You have to decide what kind of man you want to be, Sid had said; and what Tony wanted was not to be this man: the bad father. He was a bad enough father back when Malcolm simply had a drinking problem, and then a drug problem. "It's my fault," Tony had said at first. "It's not your fault," people kept telling him. But they didn't know what Tony knew: after Malcolm had been living with them for a year, he broke his arm, and the doctor in Bergerac said, "This is an arm that has been broken often." Tony was more surprised by the doctor's anger than the sentence. The doctor turned to Malcolm, and said, "Who? Your father?" *No, no,* said Malcolm—of course his stepfather had done it, who else?—and Tony had said, *Why didn't you tell me?* And Malcolm had answered, "I did. Daddy, I did."

His son was going to sell the house. No rotten gift of a car would ever have stopped it.

Like Izzy, he was giving up hope. It was a physical process, the hope a sort of shrapnel working its way out of his skin. It hurt. He'd hoped Malcolm wouldn't do this, but he would, and three hundred euro for a piece-of-shit car wouldn't save them.

He, Tony, was drunk. Was he drunk? He was dizzy.

He was in the barn. The car was running. He'd meant to

turn it off. The parrot: the parrot stood on the passenger seat, heavy-eyed and gray. Tony tried the door. The handle didn't work. "Still!" said Tony. He rushed to the other side. By the time he had scooped her up, she seemed to be in a faint, if birds could faint. They stumbled out into the air together.

"Clothilde," he said, and then, longingly, "Birdie, birdie." She was burrowing into his armpit. "Breathe. Breathe."

She was still alive. Maybe the air would revive her entirely. Maybe she'd be brain-damaged: she would have lost her English and most of her French, she would only be able to say, *Olivier. Olivier. Je t'aime.* He knew nothing about the neurology of parrots. She was alive. He would take her in any condition.

Sid's truck came flying around the corner, past the mailbox into the courtyard. They were sitting three abreast, and the woman, who sat by the window, looked appalled. The order seemed wrong to Tony. He wasn't sexist, but with two men and a woman, the woman should sit in the middle, by the gearshift. Then he saw that she was driving. Of course: they were in Sid's old English right-hand-drive truck. She'd told him he was too drunk to drive. An American would think so.

Sid tumbled from the truck as though kicked. Then the woman got out the other side, and Tony saw that she was heavily pregnant. Her husband followed her. "Fucking horrible," said the husband. That's right: only the woman was American. The husband was English, and drunk as Sid. Well, if they were friends of Little Aussie Peter, of course he would be. The wife wore somebody else's Wellington boots, a plaid skirt, and a striped sweater. She had red hair and no eyebrows and kept nearly losing the wellies in the mud. The man was wearing a denim jacket and blue jeans. He sat on the front bumper of Sid's truck. He didn't look at her. It hadn't occurred to Tony until this moment that anyone willing to buy a three-hundred-euro car had to be as desperate and skint as he was. He wondered if it were even safe for a pregnant woman to ride in that car.

They had some terrible story, too, or soon would. He wished he found this realization ennobling, but he didn't: he was furious at them for whatever sadness they'd already experienced, whatever tragedy was just a headlight glow on the road ahead.

They would buy the car. He would sell it to them. That would be part of the story, anyhow.

Somewhere in England Malcolm was saying, *I should never have come here.*

He was saying, *It's too expensive.*

He was saying, *I wish it hadn't come to this, but what else can I do?*

He was talking to strangers, hoping they would absolve him. They are the only ones who ever can.

"Hi!" said the pregnant woman. "I hear you have a car?"

"I love you," said the parrot, and then, "Forgive me."

Hungry

The grandmother was a bright, cellophane-wrapped hard candy of a person: sweet, but not necessarily what a child wanted. She knew it, too. That sad bicentennial summer, her son in the hospital recovering from surgery, she and her granddaughter looked for comfort all over Des Moines: at the country club, the dinner club, the miniature-golf-course snack bar, the popcorn stand at the shopping mall, the tea room at Younkers, every buffet, every branch of Bishop's Cafeteria. What the girl liked best: to choose your own food, not just chocolate cream pie but a particular, considered wedge. To stand before the tall, toqued brunch chef, who minted Belgian waffle after Belgian waffle and rendered them unto you. The world of heat-lamped fried chicken and tall glasses of cubed Jell-O and dinner rolls with pats of butter so refrigerated you had to warm them in the palm of your hand before they'd spread. The girl had already split one pair of pants. It hadn't seemed to bother her. "Oh, well," she'd said, reaching around to verify the rend. "Never mind."

Now here was Lisa, aged ten, the morning of the Fourth of July, 1976, zaftig, darling, oblivious, dressed for the occasion as some founding father: navy polyester pants knickerbockerishly tucked into tube socks, a pair of red and white espadrilles that had run in the rain, a thin ruffled lavender shirt borrowed from Sylvia herself. The outfit showed every ounce the girl had put on in the past month. She'd come from Boston to be taken care of while her father was in the hospital. Instead, the two of them had eaten all the things Aaron—sweet Aaron, the grandmother's oldest—could not.

"Who are you, sweetheart?" Sylvia asked. "George Washington?"

"Patrick Henry!" said Lisa. "I'm going to perform his Glorious Speech at the block party."

"You're going to what?"

The girl began to hunt through the fruit bowl in the middle of the dining-room table. "I have it memorized. I did it for the fourth-grade talent show."

"Did you win?"

"Did I *win*?" Lisa thumbed a grape loose from its fellows and chewed it. "It wasn't a contest," she said at last. "People clapped."

"I don't understand," said Sylvia. "You want to say the speech at the party? You can't just start shouting."

"I won't shout."

"You can't just make everything stop so people will look at you," said Sylvia.

"Oh," said Lisa, "you'd be surprised." She pinched off another grape and ate it.

The fruit bowl was an attempt to offset the buffets. Aaron wouldn't mind, probably, nor his wife, Marjorie, who was herself plump, but if Aaron's sister found out that their mother had overseen a noticeable weight gain—well, Rena had already suggested that Sylvia was responsible for Aaron's bad heart, even though their father, Sylvia's husband, had his first heart attack even earlier, at forty-two, and had died of his third twenty years later. According to Rena, their childhood had been one long period of Sylvia like a mad bomber installing explosives in the bodies and souls of her children, set to go off when they became adults. Sylvia wondered how long it might take to return Lisa to her original condition.

Sylvia still filled the candy dish in Lisa's room, but with dietetic caramels and sugar-free fake M&M's. She bought a brand of soda pop called Kalorie Kounter, in cans festooned with tape measures that floated like banners in an old oil painting. For the block party this afternoon, she and Lisa together had made a lo-cal noodle kugel: low-fat cottage cheese, fat-free sour cream, margarine, a cornflake topping.

Terrible, unutterable words: *fattening, lo-cal, dietetic*. And anyhow, every day Mrs. Tillman across the hall called Lisa over and fed her orange marshmallows shaped like enormous peanuts, and Pixy Stix. Lisa's first day in Des Moines, Mrs. Tillman had knocked on the apartment door. "I have suckers," she'd said. "You have what?" asked Sylvia. "Suckers, suckers," said Mrs. Tillman, digging in the pockets of her housecoat. When she pulled out her hand, she'd caught a number of lollipops between her knuckles by the sticks. All yellow. Either they were cheaper to buy that way or she'd already eaten the good colors herself.

Thereafter Lisa went to visit Mrs. Tillman every morning. "She loves it here," Mrs. Tillman always said, a note of competition in her voice. Mrs. Tillman's late husband had owned an appliance store, and she had retained an appliance-like air, functional, awkward, a woman to be moved around on a dolly. *I am the grandmother,* Sylvia thought but didn't say. *That is the winning hand. That beats all other old ladies, no matter what.* Then she and Lisa would go out and flag the ice-cream truck. Fudgsicle for Lisa, Dreamsicle for her.

"Why don't you do the speech for me?" Sylvia asked Lisa now. She sat down on the sofa, her hands clasped. "Then you can just enjoy the party."

"No, thanks. Daddy says I should save it for the performance."

"What performance?"

The girl shrugged. "He taught me Hamlet's speech to his players, too. 'Speak the speech, I pray you.'" Another grape. This one she tossed in the air: it bounced off her chin. "Oops. Anyhow, it was his idea, when I told him about the party. So I better."

"He doesn't understand—"

"Grandma," the girl said seriously. "You have to do what sick people ask."

In earlier years, Sylvia had been a one-foot-in-front-of-the-other person. When disasters happened (her mother had taught her) you strode firmly in the opposite direction, because calamity followed catastrophe followed disaster. People who believed things couldn't get worse were the ones who were killed, by man or nature. You had to get away.

But the Bicentennial summer, all she could think was, *my fault*. She could hardly move for culpability. That's what happened when you were the oldest surviving member of your family. You could not cast blame any further back: it was yours, like your spinster aunt's diploma. Everyone else refused it, and the only way to hand it down was to die.

She'd fed that boy, her son, too well. That's what Rena said: she'd starved the girl and stuffed the boy. Last Thanksgiving Rena had come with her steno notebook full of all the ways that Sylvia had damaged her, as though at the end she might present her mother with a bill. *Distrust of men*: $9,000. *Fear of living alone*: $15,000. "I need to do this," said Rena, and she flipped page after page and listed injury: how Sylvia and Ben had always taken Aaron more seriously; how in the family you had to be careful about hurting men's feelings but women didn't matter; how they hadn't bought her a piano when that was all she really wanted. Aaron wanted a dog, he got a dog. Aaron wanted a car, he got a car.

"I don't remember you ever asking!" Sylvia had said.

"You knew," said Rena darkly. Then she added, "You never loved me unconditionally. There were always strings."

"What are you talking about? Darling, I absolutely loved you. *Love* you."

"You didn't love me the way you loved Aaron."

What could Sylvia say? That was true. Not more nor less but differently. If one could measure love—but even then love was too various, one love would have to be measured by degrees Fahrenheit and one by atomic weight. First born, second, boy, girl: of course different loves. To compare was nonsense. What Rena wanted: scales with packages of maternal love, finally squared—but then she'd complain about something else. *You just gave me the same love you'd already given Aaron! You didn't treat me like an individual!*

A different love for grandchildren, too: unreserved. Gleeful. Greedy. Sylvia was allowed to rub Noxzema into Lisa's sunburnt back after a day at the swimming pool. She let Lisa pick out expensive shampoo at the grocery store, something called Milk Plus that smelled like the 1930s baby soap she'd washed her children with. So what if Lisa'd fallen asleep with the bubble gum they got from the candy store, and it ended up in her hair and had to be cut out? They walked down to Sal's salon, and now Lisa had her first real haircut from a professional. They cuddled on the orange guest bed and watched television and ate popcorn. Oh, if Rena ever found out how Sylvia loved the childish flub of her granddaughter, the dense bakery heat of her limbs, her neck like a loaf of bread—a voracious love, a near starvation though here the girl was in front of her. That was what the love of children was like, in Sylvia's experience, and she supposed it made sense that Rena was sad that such mother love had to end, to mellow. You couldn't bite a grown-up. You couldn't sniff at an adult woman's neck. If she went to Rena's therapist—that was who had insisted on the steno pad, the formal accusation—she surely would have hated to hear what it meant, her longing to bite children. To devour them. She nibbled, she tickled, she nuzzled, she inhaled. That was the real end of childhood, wasn't it, when you looked at a stringy kid and loved her but didn't want to bite.

But it pained her, too, the pudge of her granddaughter's thighs. The straps of her bathing suit cut into her shoulders, and her face had changed. She'd been so casual about the split pants, as though it happened all the time. At ten, weight didn't matter so much, and of course, a smart girl like that was more than her body. Rena had said, *You made it seem as though your love for me was dependent on my weight!* No, of course not. A mother loves her children no matter what. *But* other *people, darling Rena,* she wanted to say, *other people* do *care, other people might well love you less.* Her job as a mother—she believed this then, believed it now—was to make sure that her children would be loved by the maximum number of other people. This was the source of all of her anxiety.

They would get the weight off before it was time for Lisa to go home, she'd decided. Surely that was possible.

. . .

They were getting ready to leave for the block party when the phone rang.

"Hold on!" Sylvia called. The nearest phone was in the kitchen.

"I'm going to see Mrs. Tillman," Lisa said, and Sylvia tried to give her a wave that said both *all right* and *don't ruin your lunch*.

"Mama," said Rena on the phone. "I need you to be calm. All right?" But Rena's own voice was not calm. Sylvia took off her sunglasses and replaced them with her indoor ones. She sat at the kitchen table. The phone cord just reached.

"Mama," said Rena. "It's Aaron. Mama, things do not look good."

The clock on the kitchen wall was shaped like a frying pan. Why on earth, Sylvia wondered, what could it mean, a clock like a skillet?

"He's on a ventilator," said Rena. "But—they'll take him off it. This afternoon, probably."

A heart attack, a little heart attack, like his father's first one. A good heart attack, the kind that could scare you into behaving. Sylvia cleared her throat. "And then what happens?" she asked.

Rena let out a long rattling noise, halfway between a sigh and a moan, which Sylvia understood as another accusation of maternal crime.

"Mama—"

"What do the *doctors* say?"

"Well, he'll stop breathing," said Rena. "So."

"I'll call the airline," said Sylvia. "I'll hurry. Lisa's—no, we'll drive to the airport right now—"

"We need you to stay there," said Rena.

"We? Who?"

"I've talked to Marjorie. That's what she wants."

"Where are you?"

"I'm here at the hospital. I drove up last night, when things started to look bad."

"Rena!" said Sylvia, and now she was standing up, the phone cord wrapped around her hand (that twisted, loved, comforting phone cord, like a length of worry beads). "Rena, of course I have to be with him, I *have* to—"

"Mom," said Rena. "No."

"I can help! If she'll let me! *Aaron,*" said Sylvia, as though that was the problem, a mother needed to say her dying child's name aloud, to call him back to life.

"This isn't about you," said Rena, in her kindest voice.

Well, who was it about, then? That was the thing: Rena always remembered that Sylvia was their mother but somehow forgot that this meant they were Sylvia's children.

"And you *can* help," said Rena. "Keep Lisa with you, and happy. Tomorrow—when it's over, it would be wonderful if you could bring her home. All right?"

"What do I tell her?" said Sylvia.

"Nothing. That's very important, Mom. All right? Marjorie needs to figure out what to say. *She's* the mother."

"All right," said Sylvia. "OK. You'll call me?"

And then Rena's voice fully broke, and she said, "Of course. You'll be the first one. I'll see you soon."

. . .

There were only eight units in the building, all with the same floor plan, identical or mirrored, depending. To see what other people did with their apartments was disconcerting, a separated-at-birth moment. Your life would look like this, if you weren't you. She could hear dim mechanical sounds inside Mrs. Tillman's apartment after she'd rung the bell. What was her first name, anyhow? Sylvia imagined a tag on her that said (like her husband's goods) TILLMAN. That's what brand of woman she was. Sylvia was doing her best not to cry. She had a few seconds more of doing her best on her own.

The door opened to reveal Mrs. Tillman, behind her a wall of hung decorative plates, each with a scene of Hummels through the seasons. China plates with china figurines. Sylvia was panting, she realized.

Then she reminded herself that she had a job: to keep Lisa happy.

"Ah!" said Tillman. Her hair was coral-colored. She leaned on a walker that seemed too short for a tall woman. It gave her a restrained look, as a lunatic is restrained in a sanitarium. "Hello, Syl. We had a little problem."

Sylvia wondered, for a moment, whether Mrs. Tillman had had a stroke; then she saw that she'd merely applied her lipstick off-center.

"We had a little problem," Mrs. Tillman repeated. "We used something without permission. Talcum powder." She gestured at a dusty-headed, teary-eyed Lisa, who stood by a garish bird-patterned sofa. *Lisa knows,* thought Sylvia. *How does she know?*

"I wanted to look like I had a powdered wig," said Lisa.

"Ah!" said Sylvia. "Did you say you were sorry, darling?"

Lisa nodded.

"So we had a little spank," said Tillman in a bright voice, "and now we are friends again."

A little . . . spank? Sylvia tried to make sense of this. Tillman nodded encouragingly, and then mock-spanked the back of her own wrist, to illustrate.

"You *spanked* her?" Sylvia looked at the plates again and saw them for what they were: portraits of children who in five years would join the Hitler Youth, little lederhosened, dirndled monsters. She wanted to pluck the plates one by one from the wall and smash them, and then she realized the strange feeling in her arms was her hands, which were heavy as sandbags and had been since she'd hung up the phone. Grief had made them huge. They felt ready to drop off her wrists. Lisa couldn't get out, not past the walker, which seemed not the support of an elderly woman but a torture device to be used on small children. Sylvia reached over and picked the walker up and moved it closer to Tillman's body.

"Syl!" said Tillman, stumbling back, and so Sylvia grabbed her by the wrist. The other hand she held out for Lisa, who took it and was out of the apartment and under her grandmother's wing, smelling of ticklish, tickling babyhood.

"Are you crazy?" Tillman said. "Let go!"

Sylvia was still holding Tillman's wrist. She felt she could snap it. The ulna of a Hummel: of course china people had china bones.

"I'll call the police!" said Tillman.

"*You?*" said Sylvia. "Call them! I'll have you arrested!"

"You're hurting me! Let go!"

"Call the police!" Sylvia said. "You don't *spank* some-one else's child! Nobody's! It's barbaric!"

"Grandma," said Lisa. "It didn't even hurt! Please!"

Sylvia flung Tillman's wrist back at her, and the door closed. From the other side they heard Tillman say, "The police? You call the police on me, I'll call them on you!" A thud: she must have struck the inside of her door; then they heard the chain lock slide closed.

They stood in the hallway together, Sylvia and Lisa, not yet bereaved.

"Let's just get out of here," said Lisa. "Let's go to the party. Let's go the back way."

Poor girl, thought Sylvia, but she meant herself.

She was returning to her body. Her hands still felt over-sized, but filled with helium. All she really wanted was to go to her apartment, to her bedroom, to the back of her walk-in closet, to sit among the shoes. She thought she might feel better if she gnawed on one.

No. They had to keep busy. That was the only way they might manage. She didn't know what a ventilator was, exactly. Did it go over your face? Down your throat? When-ever she heard the words *life support* she pictured a series of cords attached all over a sick person's body, all leading to one enormous plug in the wall: that was the plug that was pulled, when you pulled the plug. Suddenly she understood life support as something that involved a certain amount of brute force. A shim, a brace. The phone might be ringing in her apartment even now. They walked away, down the back steps. When her children were little and first came home from school to tell her things they'd learned—for instance, that Ponce de León had come to the United States on Columbus's second voyage—she'd always felt unnerved: they knew things she didn't. Now they still did. Aaron would die. He would die. (She repeated this in her head a few more times.) And apparently this death was not about her and not about Lisa.

They were outside now, in the sun. The street smelled of gunpowder and lemonade. Little kids held their hands in the bright showers off sparklers. Everyone else was in shorts and sleeveless shirts, Sylvia saw. Nobody else was in costume.

"Don't eat anything with mayonnaise," she told Lisa.

"Because it's fattening?"

"It goes bad in the heat. You could die from hot mayonnaise. No potato salad. Listen, darling. It isn't right that Mrs. Tillman spanked you. No one has the right to spank you, you understand?"

Lisa nodded seriously. Then she said, "Can you fix my queue?"

"Your what, darling?"

"My pigtail." The girl turned and presented her back. Sylvia tightened the sad braid, the brown hair slippery under the talc, faded, like a sun-damaged photo. The bow was blue. Her shoulders were broad. Sylvia stroked them. Without turning around, Lisa said, "My dad spanks me sometimes."

"Well," said Sylvia, shocked, "did you deserve it?"

But Lisa was already hopping away on her smudged espadrilles towards the dessert table.

She came back with a cream puff—cream puffs! worse than tuna salad!—and with Bill Antoni, the superintendent of the building, a retired custodian. He and his wife lived in the basement, next to the all-purpose room and the storage lockers. He was wearing a tank top that said FORD across the chest, the word buckled by the curve of his belly. Even from this distance, the mustache that hid his upper lip looked dirty.

"George Washington here has a question for you!" he said to Sylvia.

"Patrick Henry," said Lisa.

Sylvia looked at Lisa, as seriously as she could: as much seriousness as Lisa could hope for herself, or for Patrick Henry. "What is it, sweetheart?"

"Can I have a sparkler?"

"Of course."

"Told ya," said Bill Antoni. He smiled at Sylvia, with a little wink like an afterthought.

Should she tell him? A mad spanker in the building. Surely he should know, so he could attend to it, the way he attended to the furnace and the landscaping. But she felt the moment she opened her mouth she would unravel, tell him everything, fall into his arms. Bill Antoni's mustache was nostril-damp in two channels. He was fat, healthy, alive. The sound of a police siren came winding from the distance, and Sylvia wondered whether it had been hailed by Tillman, coming for her.

Bill Antoni handed Lisa the thin wire of the unlit sparkler. "Hold steady. That's it. Hey, there's going to be dancing later."

Lisa stared at the spot where the stick met Bill Antoni's
flame, and said, "I don't dance," and Sylvia thought that
was the saddest thing she'd ever heard, and besides, *Don't
stare at fire.*

The sparkler caught. Lisa held on to it with both
hands, as though it were a responsibility, not a pleasure.
Yes, thought Sylvia: *my fault, my fault.* She had made
Aaron, and Aaron had made Lisa (though Sylvia herself
had no sense of being made by her parents, only loved). If
Rena had been there with the steno pad, Sylvia would have
signed it, like a confession, and demanded, at last, her punishment. Surely her crimes were capital. She wished to burn
like the sparkler, beautifully, fatally. They all watched.

When it sputtered out, Bill Antoni said to Lisa, "What
do you mean, you don't dance?"

"I'm more into forensics," she said.

He scratched his head with the hand that held the
lighter. "Like dead people?"

"Speeches. I give speeches. I'm going to give one today. I
have it memorized."

Sylvia thought this would put an end to it. Bill Antoni
would make it clear: this is a block party, not a debate meet,
you strange, strange child.

"Well, why not?" he said. "Come this way. That all right
with you, Grandma?"

I am not your grandma, thought Sylvia, but she nodded.
A moment to breathe. A moment to herself. "Right, then,"

said Bill Antoni, and he led Lisa away, and Sylvia knew she'd made a mistake. She never wanted a moment alone for the rest of her life.

The last time she'd seen Aaron in person had been at Thanksgiving, in Boston, ice on the ground; on this day he was dying, it was hot; which would she remember?

They should be inside, to answer the phone. They should be out here, in order not to. She pictured the phone ringing and ringing, Rena forced to stand by one of the hospital payphones, thinking of her mother, cursing her, "Mom, come on, answer," and Sylvia wanted to fold that girl in her arms, too, the one about to lose her brother, my God, there was no loss like that, was there. Sylvia had gone through it herself with her sisters. Aaron's eyes were violet and his hair was black. Had been black before it turned silver. That was why she should be with him now, to see the actual person she was losing, though of course she was losing every version of him: the daredevil baby, the thoughtful ten-year-old, the know-it-all teenager.

There was nothing she could do. She was not in Boston. She could only take care of the girl in Des Moines. As long as they were out here, among the slaws and the Jell-O and the burnt hot dogs, the beguiling array of potato chips, the flags attached to tricycles, made into bunting. Out here Lisa was not fatherless and Sylvia was not sonless. Aaronless. They hadn't yet sustained that particular damage. Damage: a Rena word, as though any of us made it through life in mint condition. But surely some things were worse than others. As long as Lisa didn't know, she was still perfect. Flawless.

Where was she?

There. In fact, someone *had* put up a little stage, and Lisa was on it. That haircut Sal had given her was terrible, long in back, layers in the front where the gum had been. The talc at her temples was runneled with sweat. She seemed to have dropped a pickled beet down the ruffles of her patriot's shirt. Her eyes were closed.

She was delivering the speech.

A small crowd was listening. A few grandmothers, some of the littler kids. Bill Antoni. An approving man in his thirties who looked like a teacher. It was so hot you could hear the mayonnaise go bad, but there was Lisa, gesturing, serious, saying, "They tell us, sir, that we are weak." July 4, 1976, 43rd Street, Des Moines, Iowa: this girl could start a revolution. Not with her good looks—though look at her, the beauty!—nor with her smarts, but because she is loved, she is loved, she is—Sylvia regarded Lisa's audience and tried to put this thought in their heads.

Because wasn't that easier? To change a dozen strangers than a single beloved? Look at this wonderful girl. Yes, thought Sylvia, she'd take the blame but she also demanded some credit.

A teenage boy glanced up, saw Lisa, and snorted.

"But as for me," she said, she was pounding her fist in her hand, she believed every word, "give me liberty, or give me death!"

—it was never that easy though, was it, to demand a choice. Ask and ask. You might want both. You might get neither.

The Lost & Found Department
of Greater Boston

Once upon a time a woman disappeared from a dead-end street. Her name was Karen Blackbird. She was a skinny, cheerful, nervous woman with muddy circles under her eyes and kinky, badly kept light-brown hair. She was five-foot-one or five-two or five-three. She had a tattoo shaped like a cherub that only a few people knew about, and a bit of pencil point in the palm of her right hand that she'd got as a kid tripping up a flight of stairs. She liked to show it to the children at the school where she worked as a lunch lady. "I could have got lead poisoning," she said, fingers spread to flatten out her hand. "No, you couldn't've," the sixth-graders said, and some of the smarter fifth-graders, "pencils aren't really made of lead, they're made of graphite." Still, they liked to look at the X-ray gray speck that broke her life line in half. The children knew nothing about palmistry, little about life, less about love, but they believed in life lines and love lines the way they believed in mercury thermometers: they meant something but probably you needed a grown-up to read them. "It means I'll write my own fate," Karen Blackbird would have said, if asked. The children, including her own son, didn't care that Karen Blackbird was forty-two: all of adulthood seemed one un-differentiated stretch of time. But the ages of objects excited them. When Karen Blackbird disappeared, the graphite in her palm was thirty-three years old.

In this case and no other, *Once upon a time* means *Late summer, 1982.*

Before her disappearance, Karen Blackbird lived in a ramshackle Victorian with her elderly father and teenage son. The son was seventeen but small: five-foot tall and eighty pounds. He hired himself out to rake leaves and shovel snow, he delivered the weekly *Graphic*—all the usual local-boy jobs. With his dark hair and his newsprint eyes, he looked like an enterprising orphan, though he dressed like a hippie, in jeans faded to gray and ragged slogan T-shirts. The grandfather didn't approve of how his daughter was raising his grandson. He believed childhood was the furnace in which men were forged: it couldn't be lukewarm. The grandfather had a head shaped like a bellows, wide at the temples, ears attached at slants, face narrowing down to a mean, disappointed, huffing mouth.

Look here: Karen Blackbird is standing on the front porch before she disappears. The house itself is a wreck, the brown asbestos tile weathered in teary streaks. A lawnmower skulks up to its alligatorish eyebrows in the yard. Half the teeth in the porch railing have been punched out, and Karen Blackbird puts the toe of her shoe through a gap in the railing and pivots her foot back and forth, as though it's a switch that might work a decision. Her loopy hair shifts in the wind. Her lips are chapped, as usual. She has the kind of face that makes old women say, "Dear, if you just took a little care, you'd be so pretty." Those old women are wrong. Her bare calves are thick and muscular, but her hands are bony. She's still too young to carry that nose with any authority. Her oversized coat is missing half its buttons. She's unlucky with buttons, always has been.

The lives of the missing begin *Last seen,* and for a moment, or a week, or a day—who knows how long—she's here. This isn't the last time. She's about to go but not right now. Only in magic shows does anyone announce the imminent disappearance of a woman. Even then you don't know what you'll find in her place.

Once upon a time—specifically, Tuesday, September 7, 1982—Asher Blackbird, last year's straight-A student, got caught trying to shoplift frozen French bread pizzas. He'd already slipped one box down the front of his hooded sweatshirt and was leaning over a freezer chest in the middle aisle of the Hi-Lo Market when he was spotted by the store manager, who took him to the back, through the silver doors with the high, round windows and the floor-sweeping brown-gray fringe at the bottom.

The Hi-Lo was a run-down, bare-bones concern with more fruit flies than customers. Anyone with a car went to the Purity Supreme a mile away. The Hi-Lo was where kids got sent by parents on orders to buy cartons of milk. If there was change, they fed the coins into the gumball and prize machines at the front of the store, the heaviest machinery they'd ever operated by themselves. Broke, they fiddled with the big, cold silver keys that worked the machines and hopefully lifted the metal doors over the chutes. They stole things: candy, the terrible toys in the terrible toy section, the school-supply kits with pygmy plastic rulers and pug-nosed scissors. They drank coffee milk in the parking lot, sitting on the concrete blocks at the ends of spaces.

"Wow!" Asher Blackbird said when the Hi-Lo manager pulled him into the back office. "OK!" He was smiling with nerves. The room smelled like a defrosted deep freeze. Asher wiped his hand across his face again and again, but the smile stayed where it was. He was clean enough but skinny, with thick black hair that looked like it had been cut in the dark. The Hi-Lo manager felt like giving him five bucks to run over to Salvi's in the next block. A boy needed a barber. "I'm sorry," said the kid. He grinned like he couldn't believe his luck.

"Sit down," said the Hi-Lo manager. He was trying to stay stern. When kids stole, he scared the hell out of them, then sent them home without calling their parents. But that was always dumb stuff—candy, toys, soda pop. Not food you had to cook. The Hi-Lo manager dropped the pizza box on the desk. On the front, two French bread pizzas were staggered on a wooden cutting board. The boy raised his eyes. Probably he came from the tenement apartments in the next block, over George's Tavern and Mac's Smoke

Shop. Maybe his mother put him up to it. It was a school day. The kid should be in school.

"How old are you?" asked the Hi-Lo manager.

"Seventeen," Asher Blackbird answered. Then he looked at the box on the desk again, smiling at the pizzas as though they were coconspirators.

A liar and *a thief, poor kid,* thought the Hi-Lo manager, *and not very clever at either.* No way was this little kid seventeen. Twelve, tops. The Hi-Lo manager himself was forty-four years old, bald, and pink, with a head dented like the cans in his store and an ex-wife he still loved, who still loved him, though she had remarried and had a baby. When the baby grew up, he thought, she'd divorce her husband, the fake husband, the shadow husband, and remarry him. It was the only thing that kept him in this town, where she lived; it was the only thing that kept him on this earth. She'd been his first and only girlfriend. *If I'm not married when I'm forty,* he'd told himself at twenty-seven, before he met her, *I'll kill myself.* As it turned out, he wasn't married at forty but he had been. Some days he wondered if he were breaking a vow with himself. At the Hi-Lo he wore a short-sleeve shirt and a red knit necktie and an engraved name tag that said VAL.

"Your mother home now?" he asked.

That took the smile off the boy's face. "No," he said.

"Where is she? Work?"

The boy looked at him again, and the Hi-Lo manager saw something else. He couldn't put his finger on it, though later he'd decide it was grief.

"How about your father?" he asked. "Sisters? Brothers?"

Asher Blackbird looked down. "No," he said at last. His hands were on his knees—huge hands, the Hi-Lo manager saw then. Big feet, too, like a rottweiler puppy. "Just my grandfather."

"Wait here," said the Hi-Lo manager. Outside the swinging doors, a mustached policeman flirted with Marietta from the meat department as she lay down minute steaks in the case. The Hi-Lo manager didn't trust policemen who flirted. At the deli counter, he grabbed a piece of the awful fried chicken from the hot box, a few of the soda-heavy biscuits, a carton of milk. When he brought them back, the boy was holding the unopened pizza box in his lap and shaking it.

"You hungry?" asked the Hi-Lo manager. "It's all right. Here."

Asher Blackbird was already eating the chicken. "I'm a vegetarian," he said apologetically between bites. Beneath its brown coating, the chicken meat looked indecent. The Hi-Lo manager handed him a paper napkin folded into thirds.

He stepped outside to talk to the flirtatious policeman, and Asher Blackbird gnawed on the beveled cartilage at the end of the bone. He chewed and chewed and then threw up in the wastebasket by the desk. After wiping his mouth he started on the biscuits.

Officer Leonard Aude drove Asher Blackbird home. Aude had offered the front seat of the cruiser, but the boy said he'd rather ride in back. In the rearview mirror, the kid looked even younger. "You OK there?" Aude asked.

"Yes, sir."

"Which house? Buddy? Which one."

Asher Blackbird kept raising and lowering the hood of his sweatshirt. "That one. The brown. Brownish."

"Your ma's not home, you said. Where is she?"

After a long pause, the boy said, "I don't know. Gone. She's just—gone."

"Yeah? Since when?"

"Don't know. Six months?"

"Six? Who else you live with?"

"Nobody."

"Your mother left you alone?"

"No," said the boy. Aude could hear him playing with the zipper of his jacket. "I live with my grandfather," he said finally.

Aude looked at the house, the garbage on the porch, the soggy gray newspapers on the steps, the advertising fliers sticking out of the wall-mounted mailbox. A wind-twisted, unhinged storm door leaned against the porch balustrade.

"He's Blackbird, too, right? Nathan. That him?"

The boy didn't seem surprised that Aude had heard of his grandfather. "That's him," he said.

"And how is it, living with your grandfather?"

The boy shrugged, shook his head. "I can't," he said finally.

"OK, buddy," said Leonard Aude. "We're gonna take care of you. Be right back."

Inside the house, Aude's boat-size heart sunk: he could

feel it take on weight and drop. That's what happened when you got smacked in the face with how people lived. No one was taking care of the boy. He'd be going into Social Services and the mother arrested when she showed back up. The house smelled of garbage and cats, though only one cat was visible, asleep on a ladder-back chair. It lifted its head. A line of drool trailed down from its mouth. Aude hadn't known cats could drool. It needed a good home, too.

"Hello?" he called.

The whole living-room ceiling looked ready to collapse from damp. Five different wallpaper patterns were peeling off the wall. Scattered around the main room were half-filled cardboard boxes that looked slept on—coming in? going out?—and a sunroom beyond seemed an asylum for insane and injured furniture. In the cave-like kitchen, Aude noticed that every single cabinet was secured with bicycle locks. Some of the chains were thick; others narrow, candy-colored, plastic-wrapped. That, he was certain, was the work of Nathan Blackbird.

Aude climbed the stairs. Later he'd be furious, but for the moment he felt only the deep sorrow that visited him whenever he got someplace later than he should have, when he saw how helpless the world was, eventually, to protect its children. The carpet runner under his feet was as filthy as a garage floor. At the top he turned and walked down the hall. A voice muttered behind a door.

"Hello? Mr. Blackbird," said Aude.

The voice muttered on.

Aude opened the door and peered in. Compared to the

rest of the house, the room was oddly tidy. A window air conditioner chugged away. The dresser beneath was glazed with dust. The head end of the old iron sleigh bed had been raised on books: under one side, the Boston yellow pages and *A–Ak* of *The Book of Knowledge*, a premium from the Purity Supreme. Under the other, the white pages and *XYZ*.

Ordinarily, Nathan Blackbird would have confessed to everything. He was a confessor. That's why he was known to the police. Before he'd come to live with Karen and Asher, he'd been in a boardinghouse with other old men. Twice a year he'd show up at the station, offering up his wrists and claiming he'd murdered someone. He never had. He wanted incarceration, blame, absolution—what anybody ever wanted—but he was too chickenshit to do anything to earn them. *At last,* he would have said to Leonard Aude, had he noticed him there, *finally you believe me. I'm the Boston Strangler. I'm the San Andreas Fault.*

The head of the bed had been raised to improve Nathan Blackbird's circulation, though his circulation had stopped two days before, when he'd had a heart attack in his sleep. His arms were outside of the bedclothes; his wrists touched at the pulse points as if he were again, as always, ready for handcuffs.

"Aw, shit, Nathan," said Aude to the corpse. "Mr. Blackbird, dammit."

The back of the body would be black with pooled blood, a half-swamped boat, but what was visible was pale and so far intact, thanks to the chill of the room. The muttering voice came from a police scanner on the bedside table: Nathan Blackbird liked to listen to reports of all the crimes he didn't commit. Aude turned it off so he wouldn't have to hear himself radio in. Then he went to talk to the kid.

Once upon a time a woman disappeared from a dead-end street. Nobody saw her go. She must have stepped out the door of the Victorian she shared with her father and son. She must have walked down the front steps. She was accompanied or unaccompanied, willing or unwilling. She left behind her head-dented pillow like a book on a lectern, on the right page one long hair marking her place for the next time. She left behind the socks that eventually forgot the particular shape of her feet and the shoes that didn't, the brown leather belt that once described her boyish waist, dozens of silver earrings, the pajamas she'd been wearing when last seen. She left behind her mattress printed with unfollowed instructions for seasonal turning. She left behind her car. She left behind the paperback mystery she'd been reading.

She'd been fired from her job as a lunch lady at the local grade school for allowing the children to give her back rubs. She'd had a boyfriend but they'd broken up. She'd been talking religion again; there was a girl in Hamilton, Ontario, who'd suffered a head injury and was supposedly performing miracles, and Karen Blackbird had been thinking of going. All her life she'd been looking for God. She went to church services, temple, the free brunch at the International Society for Krishna Consciousness. Then she'd come home to sleep on her own doubt-scented sheets. Maybe this time she'd elected to stay among the faithful.

She left behind a basement filled with old photographs, smashed hats, a sprung wicker love seat that resembled the Brooklyn Bridge, a trunk full of bank statements, a canvas bag of orphaned keys, an asthmatic furnace, a noncommittal hot-water heater.

In the upstairs bathroom she left a disheveled toothbrush with a fleshy red rubber point at one end to massage her gums, the round lavender disposable razor that she used on her legs but not under her arms, a black rubber comb bought from a truck-stop vending machine, a blond boar bristle brush darkened with her hair.

She left behind her elderly father and her son. She never should have done that. Her father had a temper and a criminal record. The son was defenseless. He was little for his age, and then he turned sullen, and skinnier, and his skin got ashy, and he seemed barely awake in class, and everyone thought, *At last, the poor kid's going through puberty.*

But the truth was only that his grandfather was starving him to death.

A picture of Karen Blackbird appeared on the evening news. It made her inaccurately beautiful. Her hair had been pulled back and tamed along the territory of her skull. She wore dark lipstick. The flash obscured the oddness of her nose. Her paisley dress had smocking across the chest and cutouts over the shoulders. On the nearest shoulder, you could see a few freckles, the kissing kind. Maybe the coincidences of light and angle made her beautiful; maybe it was the affection of the photographer. If you went looking for the woman in the picture, you might never find the real Karen Blackbird. It was Asher Blackbird's favorite picture of his mother. He had given it to the police. They questioned him for a while, but he knew her only the way you know your mother—the smell of her, the dogleg corridors of her faith, the sloppy scrape of her left foot as she walked. Not scars, not most of her secrets.

In a house like that, how could you tell whether someone had packed for a trip, and for how long?

Had Asher known his grandfather was dead? *He slept a lot,* said the boy, *he got mad when I bothered him.* When did the chains go up? *After my mother left.* But why? *Because I was a vegetarian.* What does that have to do with anything? *My grandfather didn't believe in vegetarians: he said if I got hungry enough I'd eat what I was given.*

Why didn't you leave?

At that the boy looked confused. "I *live* there," he said at last.

Not anymore, you don't, said the police. *Don't worry, we'll find you somewhere good. Someplace that'll feed you.*

In the meantime the kid stayed with Leonard Aude and his wife. He gained ten pounds the first two weeks.

On every tree and telephone pole in the neighborhood:

HAVE YOU SEEN KAREN?

NAME: KAREN BLACKBIRD
AGE WHEN LAST SEEN: 42

HEIGHT: 5'2" (ABOUT)
WEIGHT: 100 LBS (ABOUT)

That was all. It was all the manager of the Hi-Lo Market knew. He'd Xeroxed the photo from the local paper. The library's photocopier was feeble, and Karen Blackbird looked frozen in a block of ice. He replaced the fliers every week, whether they'd been rained on or not, but forgot to include a number to call. They were like the refrain of some pop song as you passed them on the street, all question and no way to answer.

Have you seen Karen? Have you seen Karen? Have you seen Karen?

The Hi-Lo manager worked six days a week and waited for someone to come question him. No one did. Shouldn't someone have asked him what he knew? He'd found the boy, he'd alerted the police. *I could tell something was wrong, right away.* He wouldn't mention his initial anger—not that the boy was stealing, but that he was stealing so ineptly the Hi-Lo manager was obliged to collar him. He would describe the way the boy looked, hollow-eyed. *A good kid,* the Hi-Lo manager imagined saying.

Surely the Hi-Lo manager had a right. Before he found the boy, he'd had an idea that the one good thing in his life was his love for his ex-wife. Most people didn't know what that kind of love was like. He hadn't known himself back when they were married, when he felt only as though he were doing it wrong, as though there were a curtain between them. Divorce had lifted that curtain, and now when they spoke on the phone he could suddenly declare, in his truest voice, "I love you," and he could hear the breath knocked out of her, and then her answer—matter-of-fact because she couldn't deny it—"I love you, too." Then they'd just breathe at each other a while, across the perforated tops of the phones, breathe, breathe, and then she'd say, "What are you cooking yourself for dinner? Tell me." Mostly he cooked hamburgers, but he learned a few other dishes so he could tell her something else.

Then he found the boy. Shouldn't that change his life?

A locksmith replaced the front door lock of number 13, then added a hasp and a padlock. An orange-overalled man nailed a piece of plywood over the broken window. Who had hired them? One at a time, a woman, two men, and a teenage girl left funereal flowers on the front steps of the ramshackle house. Who for? No one mourned the dead man. They were ghouls, those flower leavers. They wanted to attend a funeral but there wasn't one. Nathan Black-bird's body was still waiting at the morgue for someone to claim it. The boy had been sent away to live in a new home, a clean one, in another town.

Some fool—the manager of the Hi-Lo—came with a length of yellow ribbon to tie around a tree, like with the hostages a few years back. It was still in the early years of American ribbons. He was disappointed to see that there was no tree, and besides, someone had already tied yellow ribbon—but, no, that was just police tape. The Hi-Lo manager tied his ribbon around a bush.

One of the neighbor girls came out to talk to him. She was blond and chinless and rubber-mouthed, with a thick lower lip.

"He's coming back," she said to him.

"Who?"

"Asher Blackbird."

"Yeah?" said the Hi-Lo manager.

She nodded. He had a sudden feeling of waking up in a hospital and knowing how bad your condition was by looking at your ward mates.

"You know Karen?" he asked cautiously.

She said, "Look." She was pointing to a spot above her right eye, a blue-gray shadow.

"What?" he said.

"Pencil," she said. "First day of school a kid slapped me on the back while I was erasing. Now, Karen," she said, and flipped out her palm, "had the same thing, here."

"Pencil."

"In her palm. Right on this line."

"Lana!" a woman called from the porch next door.

"Gotta go," said the girl.

A piece of pencil in her hand! In the coming months, the Hi-Lo manager would look at his own palm, expecting to see it there, a pencil point beneath the skin, twitching like a compass needle.

Suddenly everything in the neighborhood, it seemed, was lost. Telephone poles were feathered with MISSING posters until you couldn't see Karen Blackbird's face. People didn't take her down, they just tacked up their new losses over hers. Missing: A bobtailed German shepherd named Ponto. A watch with only sentimental value. A tabby cat named James who needed medication. Rodan, beloved parakeet. *Please look. Please check your basements. Have you seen me?* People wanted to help. They kidnapped the wrong animals, kept them in garages, and called phone numbers. "Are you *sure* it's not Ponto?" a worried woman asked Ponto's owner, who answered, "Lady, a dog is not a starfish. Tails do not grow back." A neighborhood away, a ten-year-old girl wrote in block letters, *Help find me! I am a German shepherd, I answer to "Auntie," I am nervous and sometimes bite.*

They found a body.

The body belonged—if that word made sense, if once you were dead your body still *belonged* to you—to a woman in her thirties or forties. She'd been lashed to a shopping cart and pushed into the Charles River. She was found three months after Karen Blackbird officially disappeared. Skeletal remains, they said. Someone had broken the dead woman's cheekbone recently, and her femur some years before. She wore a T-shirt that said VIRGINIA IS FOR LOVERS. That survived, but anything else—tattoos, a bit of pencil in the palm, signs she fought back—had been boiled off by the river. There was Karen in the newspaper again, with her freckled shoulders.

But the coroner decided the next day that the body wasn't hers; it had been in the river for a year. There was no evidence anyone had reported this particular woman missing. She'd only been found.

Someone always confesses eventually. In this case, his name was Manny Coveno. The mug shot printed in the paper convinced everyone: nose broken into several bends, a few days' growth of black beard, a mole just below his right eye that looked like a thumbprint. He'd been picked up in Providence at the end of a week of heavy drinking: he'd wandered into the lobby of the Biltmore Hotel at three A.M. shouting, "I did it! I did it! I did it!"

Even Manny didn't know what he was doing in Providence, but his confession seemed plausible. He'd known Nathan Blackbird. They'd kept rooms in a boardinghouse called the Hollis Hotel till the woman who ran it died and the property was sold. Manny, homeless, went on the march. The few people who knew him said they couldn't imagine him killing anyone. Still, he'd confessed.

He was so drunk it took him two days to sober up, at which point he went into the delirium tremens. They sent a police stenographer to take notes.

I strangled her. I stabbed her. Threw her body off the bridge. The bridge, the bridge by the trackless trolleys. Blackbird, Blackbird, Nathan Blackbird. I hated him. She took him away and I followed. She picked him up. I waited. I waited ten, eleven, fifteen years. I caught her. I caught her and I killed her.

How?

Oh, any way at all. I bit her. Nathan Blackbird. There was a guy—you can't believe the things he'd do. He's the devil. I swear to you, sir, he's the devil, and me, too.

Nathan Blackbird?

Of course. He helped me. I helped him. I bit her. I killed her.

Did you do anything else?

Plenty.

Did you rape her?

"Oh, Jesus, sir," said Manny Coveno, shocked, "I could never do a thing like that."

"Not that or the rest of it," his sister said, trying to get him released. "He's a child, he's got an IQ of sixty-eight. I'll show you his records. They loved him in school. He lost his way!"

"He lost his way, and we found him," said the police chief.

For four days Manny Coveno spoke. On TV, as he was taken from the police car to the jail, he looked less convincing, a little guy with the kind of skull-baring brush cut mothers force on their sons in the summer. But he had a lot to say. He smothered her. He shot her. *With what kind of gun?* A bullet gun. Gun that shoots bullets. He wrapped her body in a sheet and put it on a train. A boxcar. A subway. She had gone to heaven and he'd gone, too. He'd killed her with a blunderbuss. He'd killed her with a credit card. With poison. He'd hidden her under his bed, she was still there, she'd been there for ages. He had been in love with her— wasn't everyone? *In love with who, Manny?* With the girl. The girl. That girl.

On the fifth day, he woke up in his cell. His heart was calm. The walls were steady. He was astounded to hear that he'd been arrested for murder.

"Well, maybe I did it," he said to his lawyer. "I don't remember much of anything about anything."

"You didn't," said his lawyer, an awkward young woman named Slawson. She was a friend of his sister's, and she was relieved to believe he was innocent, because he terrified her.

The police had followed every single harebrained lead that Manny Coveno had given them. They'd even checked the former Hollis Hotel, much to the consternation of the new owner. It had all been nonsense. He'd hallucinated every detail.

Manny began to cry. "Jesus," he said. "Who did I kill?"

"Manny," said Slawson desperately. She felt her pockets for a handkerchief. "You didn't kill anyone."

"Then why am I here? Oh, Jesus, I don't want to kill anyone!"

"They thought you killed Karen Blackbird, but you didn't."

"Blackbird? She Nathan's wife?"

"Daughter."

"Nathan Blackbird," Manny said through his tears. "I always looked up to that guy. How's he doing?"

On the first anniversary of Karen Blackbird's disappearance—that is, the anniversary of the day he'd found Asher Blackbird—the Hi-Lo manager attended a support group for families of missing people. It was held at a junior college, in a basement classroom full of atmospheric chalk dust. Twelve people were there, sitting in chairs with paddle desks attached, and they seemed thrilled to see him.

"Who have you lost?" a kindly woman in a Red Sox cap asked.

"My wife," he answered. True enough, his ex-wife had moved the month before to Indiana, and cut off contact, though that wasn't who he was thinking of when he looked for a missing-persons support group.

The kindly woman was royalty, the mother of Deanna Manly, the teenager who in the summer of 1959 left for her job as a lifeguard at an MDC pool and vanished entirely. Despite the fact that Deanna had been missing more than twenty years, longer than she hadn't been missing, her mother wore a T-shirt bearing her daughter's face, black and white with shining hair, looking like the famous person she became that summer. BRING DEANNA HOME, the shirt said. It was well washed and worn, and the Hi-Lo manager couldn't tell what level of hope it represented.

Another woman was missing her ex-husband. She was tall and bony, with a nasal, insinuating voice and gnawed fingers. She couldn't find her ex-in-laws, either, or the ex-friends she and her ex-husband had shared, who might have died of overdoses, or probably had. They weren't in any phone book. She talked for ten minutes about how bad the marriage had been, how it had damaged her, how every day she couldn't find him was a new injury.

"It's the not-knowing that's terrible," she said.

"Excuse me," said the Hi-Lo manager.

She looked at him and stuck the side of her index finger in her mouth.

"Do you even belong here?" he asked her.

She began to nibble that finger.

"Now——" said a middle-aged man in a plaid shirt.

"Hey," said a woman next to him.

"Oh," said Deanna Manly's mother, laying her hand on the Hi-Lo manager's arm. She looked like her daughter and, despite everything that had happened, decades younger than her age; she looked, in fact, like a police artist's sketch of what Deanna would look like now, if she were alive, and for a moment the Hi-Lo manager wanted to say: *It's you, Deanna, isn't it? You're here, and your mother's missing.* "You can't question someone else's pain," she told him. "Listen. It's all valid. You can't—you can't compare one person's grief to another's."

Of course you could. Losing a fifteen-year-old daughter was worse than losing a deadbeat, drug-addicted ex-husband. He looked at the twelve people in the room: he wanted to interrogate and rank them—the married couple, the older woman with the shapes of curlers in her hair, the guy who looked like a pedophile. The finger-biter's feelings for her ex-husband were a bonsai tree—they may have started in something real, but she'd tended them so closely and for so long they were now purely decorative. Of course you could compare one person's grief to another's! All he wanted was for one single person to compare, to say to him, yes, your sadness *is* worse than anyone else's. Your sadness is inestimable.

"Do you want to tell us your story?" asked Deanna Manly's mother.

Then he remembered: he was a liar, worse than anyone.

So he told a nonsensical story stitched together from the life of Karen Blackbird, according to newspapers and magazines, and the days of his marriage. As he spoke, he believed even more strongly that there was a reason for his longing that had nothing to do with him: it was fate that had kept him from the people he loved. "She made a kind of chocolate cake with no flour," he said at last, overcome.

"Oh, yeah," said the woman with the missing ex-husband. "I make that."

"What does this have to do with you?" said the Hi-Lo manager.

Deanna Manly's mother put her hand on his arm again. "Those are wonderful, those flourless cakes. You must miss that."

He was heartbroken to hear that one of the small miracles of his marriage was a perfectly common thing.

It wasn't fair that only Karen Blackbird got a poster. Everyone wanted one.

MISSING: ONE WORLD WAR II VET, PLAYED SKY MASTERSON IN *GUYS AND DOLLS*, CAPABLE OF BENCH-PRESSING 220 POUNDS, AFFECTIONATE BUT HOTHEADED. PLEASE CALL IF SEEN.

MISSING: FAVORITE CHILD, SIX FEET TALL, MAY BE TALLER BY NOW.

MISSING, ENDANGERED: FIVE-YEAR-OLD GIRL, ONE
LAZY EYE, FASCINATED BY TYPEWRITERS, SMELLS
OF CHAPSTICK, LAST SEEN WEARING A HOSPITAL
GOWN.

The neighbors wanted stacks of MISSING posters for every person they lost, even themselves. *Missing: former self. Distinguishing marks: expectations of fame, ability to demand love. Last seen wearing: hopeful expression, uncomfortable shoes.*

"The case is still open," the police chief would say of Karen Blackbird whenever anyone asked, in a voice that suggested the case was a hole in the ground and the best they could hope for was that someone might fall in. But mostly people didn't ask. Even her son said she was a woman who could have wandered off. Not on purpose: she would have gone to the corner, leaned against a tree in the late-summer swelter. Then to the next corner, to the bus stop. She might have met someone on the bus who belonged to a church, and followed him. She might have gone all the way to Canada. So what if she'd never done it before: she was the sort of person who thought that disappointing someone was to sin against him, which was how she'd ended up pregnant, why she'd taken in her angry father. She might have acquiesced to any number of people until she was far away from home.

Let her stay lost.

For ten years, the Hi-Lo manager wondered what he would say if he saw Asher Blackbird again. *I'm glad you made it.*

I hope you're all right. Hey, son, hey, buddy: how's your life? They might bump into each other walking across the commons, or in a movie theater downtown. Not in the neighborhood, which had been razed and redeveloped, not a single old business left but the liquor store. In place of the Hi-Lo, an upscale pizza place that specialized in thin crusts; in place of the five-and-dime, one that featured deep dish. Everything gone, Mac's Smoke Shop, the Boston Fish House, the Paramount Movie Theater, George's Tavern. You couldn't even call it a neighborhood anymore. It was just office space. The Hi-Lo manager wasn't the Hi-Lo manager. He had a new job two towns over at a hardware store. He cut keys and sorted washers and was glad for the conversation: people talked in hardware stores, he found out.

Every year he went to the Blackbird place and left a bouquet on the steps. He didn't want to, he didn't even know who he was leaving the flowers for, but stopping seemed worse.

On the tenth anniversary of the day he found the boy, the Hi-Lo manager stood on the front walk of the house and looked at it: the same asbestos tile, the tilting gap-toothed porch railing. How could it have been so abandoned for so long? The neighborhood had gentrified. Even beat up, the place was worth a mint.

Then the front door opened.

A man stepped out, late twenties, with a hooked nose, wide shoulders, a tentative smile. He needed a haircut. He brushed his dark curls out of his eyes. "Can I help you?"

"Oh," said the Hi-Lo manager. He stuck the flowers be-

hind his back, like a shy suitor, and noticed that the yard
had been cleaned up, the broken window repaired. "I didn't
realize anyone lived here."

The man nodded. "Since December. Fixing it up bit by
bit. I know it doesn't look it," he said apologetically. "We're
focused on the inside. Got to do it before the baby comes.
You live on the street?"

The Hi-Lo manager nodded. "It's a good neighborhood
for kids." *Neighborhood* because he was about to say *house*
and that wasn't true: it was a catastrophic house for kids.

"I know," said the man. "I grew up here."

"In this neighborhood?"

"In this house."

Unthinkingly, the Hi-Lo manager brought around the
bouquet in its rattling cellophane, and handed it over. To
Asher Blackbird. Of course. Everything about him was different but the nose. Asher Blackbird: a grown-up. Married,
with a kid on the way. Of course he hadn't touched the outside of the house. Like the Hi-Lo manager, he hadn't given
up hope. Karen might still come back. All that ruin said,
You can always live here, if you want.

"Where have you been?" said the Hi-Lo manager, but
Asher Blackbird was turning the flowers between his palms
in a puzzled way. "Since, I mean."

"Oh. Weymouth."

"Weymouth."

"Yeah," said Asher Blackbird in an irritated voice. "I
have family there."

It was easy to be in love if you didn't declare yourself. It
was easy to be a coward. The Hi-Lo manager was lovesick,

faint. It had been years since his bodily self had been so pummeled by emotions, knees, heart, joints, stomach. He'd forgotten it was possible. He thought he might go deaf. "Asher," he said. "You don't remember me."

"Have we met?" That was familiar, too, a look on his face both damning and embarrassed.

The Hi-Lo manager said, "I'm the one who saved you."

The embarrassment evanesced. Asher Blackbird crossed his arms around the bouquet. "Saved?"

"Found."

"Leonard Aude found me."

"No," said the Hi-Lo manager.

"I talk to him all the time. I talked to him last night."

"No—before him. I'm the one who brought you to him."

"I don't know what you mean."

"At the Hi-Lo Market. I was the manager. I caught you shoplifting."

At that Asher Blackbird took a step off the porch stairs. He looked into the face of the Hi-Lo manager, who waited, waited, waited. Of course anyone's face changed over ten years. Any moment, he'd be recognized.

"I was *starving*," said Asher Blackbird at last.

"Yes, I know."

"To *death*. To actual *death*. And what did you do? You had me *arrested*. Found? *Saved*?" He lifted the bouquet like a weapon, then flung it across the yard and into the street. "Get the fuck away from me before I return the favor."

Then he was inside, the door closed behind him. A new door, the Hi-Lo manager saw now, with an oval window in it. He stood there until he saw a pale blond woman come to the door and look out.

Asher Blackbird still lives in that house. The yard is tidy, the garbage long hauled away. The neighbors have heard he's cleaned up the inside, too, painted the walls and sanded the floors and had a new kitchen put in. He'd have to, wouldn't he? All those cupboards, the chains and locks he tried to pick. Maybe he took a sledgehammer to them.

The neighbors don't know for sure. They've never been invited in, also being people who didn't save Asher Blackbird.

He and his wife have two children. The little girl sleeps in Asher's old room, and the little boy in Nathan's. Which might sound gruesome, but these are old houses. Plenty of people have died in them.

The Hi-Lo manager thinks about knocking on the door again, explaining himself, but he's waiting till he discovers the rest of the story. It's all he has to give to Asher Blackbird. So far he's leafed through descriptions of unidentified remains in thirty-seven states, files illustrated with post-mortem photos, or pencil drawings that look inhuman. *Extensive dental work. Thin gold ankle bracelet. Peach-colored brassiere, "Lovable" brand. Surgical scar. Blue T-shirt that reads,* VIRGINIA IS FOR LOVERS. *Tattoo on left buttock:* ALMA FOREVER.

Thirteen states to go. He's saving up money, having blown his budget on a psychic who told him that it was Karen who'd locked the cupboards: she'd left with her pockets full of tiny keys, scraps of paper scrawled with combinations. She'd planned to starve both of them to death. She moved to England; she has a daughter, to whom she is kind. She's remorseless.

"No," he told the psychic, "not Karen." And then, because he didn't want to hurt her feelings, "You must have looked at someone else's future."

Karen Blackbird was never seen in the neighborhood again. She was never seen anywhere again, except in California, where people see her all the time. A man grabs her arm and says, "Your family misses you, go home." But it isn't Karen Blackbird, just the actress who played her in the TV movie.

"Sorry, mister," she says.

Karen Blackbird is a mystery. Karen Blackbird is everywhere. She is alive in South America, on a sofa, dreaming of the pleasures of her son, his thick hair, his emphatic nose, his sense of humor she didn't always understand. She is dead by car crash, fire, murder, aneurysm, cancer, suicide, train wreck, drowning. She developed amnesia. She prayed for amnesia until she believed she had it. She is two mysteries at once—an open case in Massachusetts and an unidentified set of bones in a cemetery in Indiana, beneath a headstone marked JANE DOE. She is a flier that says, *Have you seen me?* and another that says, *Do you know me?* She ascended straight to heaven. She is the franking on every anonymous postcard sent anywhere.

· · ·

Once upon a time there was a mother who had an under-sized son. Sometimes even she forgot how old he really was. One night—the last night—she came into his room in her nylon pajamas. She kissed his head through his thick black hair. He was reading a book. She asked him what it was about.

"A woman miser," he said. "Her son had to get his leg amputated because she wouldn't pay for a doctor."

"That's terrible," said Karen Blackbird. She wound a lock of his hair around her finger. He swatted at her hand absentmindedly, as though it were an insect. "Well," she said, "I guess I'll go. Night, Asher B. Make sure and miss me."

On her way out she switched off the light.

"Hey!" said Asher Blackbird.

"Whoops," she said. "Force of habit." She turned to go. The pajamas were too big for her. You couldn't see the shape of her body underneath, just the tint of her skin beyond, the rolled nylon seams a shade darker, the way they hung off her. That was what he remembered later. *What color were the pajamas?* the police asked. *What sort of mood was she in?* He didn't know. Her pajamas were too big. He wished she would buy new ones.

Peter Elroy:
A Documentary by Ian Casey

"When I die," the five-year-old told his little sister, who was three, "I won't be in the forest."

"*I'm* not going die," she answered.

"You will, Jane. Nothing lasts forever."

"I'm not going *die,*" she clarified.

"When you're an old woman, you will."

"I'm not going die!"

"Jane! Listen! Calm down. It will be so, so peaceful."

But she was already crying.

Their mother called down the hall: "What's going on in there?"

"Desi says I'm going *die*!"

"Desi!"

"I didn't say *now*. But she *will* die. Everyone does!"

"I'm not going die! Mama!"

"Desi, tell your sister she's not going to die. Janie, you're not—nobody's dying."

"But—"

"Nobody's dying," their mother said firmly.

But somebody was dying, downstairs in the den that over-looked the woods behind the town house. His name was Peter Elroy, once a well-known name, still known in some circles, though never for the reasons he'd hoped. Years ago he had been the best friend of the children's father. More recently and for longer they'd been enemies. So why had he come? Because a broken promise will tie two people to-gether more surely than any ceremony.

His wife had arranged the visit, had called the boy's fa-ther to say that Peter Elroy was dying and was trying to put his affairs in order. That wasn't true. He was dying, yes, but it was his wife who was putting things in order. You needed to think of the last line of your obituary, Myra liked to say—to be fair, she'd advanced this theory before Peter's diagnosis. You want to give people hope. So she had called and extracted an invitation. She would deliver Peter and go see her sister, who lived nearby, whom Peter Elroy loathed. Evie, the sister, was made of rice pudding, body and soul. One of the things that rice-pudding Evie had once said to him: "You take up all the available oxygen in any room." Of course he did. That was how you *won*. You took up as much of the available anything as you could.

Ian wants to see you, Myra had said, and Peter Elroy

had answered, *Ian doesn't want to see me*. But his wife, who liked to make people hope, had made him hope. They got to the awful place, a duplex in a development called Drake's Landing (though there was no landing nor body of water to land from nor any interested party named Drake), only to be told that Ian Casey had been called away on business and would be back the next day. Ian's wife, who broke the news, was decades younger. She had long black hair with the kind of ragged hem that came of never having it cut. "He gives his greatest regrets," she said. "But please, come in." The note said in Ian's dyspeptic scrawl, *Sorry, sit tight and I'll be back*. The paper was now crumpled in the otherwise empty leather trash can in the corner of the den-slash-guest-room.

What was killing Peter Elroy was pancreatic cancer.

Now he sat, jilted, ditched, first by Ian and then by his own wife. When they had found out that Ian had gone, he had turned to Myra and said, "Let's go." She looked helpless, shook her head. "No, love," she said, and he understood this had never been about seeing Ian: it had been about Myra, her need for the oxygen he was always gobbling up. "I'll see you tomorrow."

His polarized glasses had turned amethyst against the sun that came through the sliding doors. Outside the house it was winter, sort of, but bright and clear, with thin snow cover that showed the pentimenti of fallen leaves and tree roots beneath it. His glasses were the opposite of the weather: overcast when it was bright, clear when it was cloudy. They suited his mood. The visiting invalid. He had been parked. Really, thought Peter Elroy, he should be in a wheelchair, with a plaid lap robe. Instead he sat on a white leather sofa whose every part seemed either to recline or slide away for storage. Everything in terrible taste, the sectional sofa (what a word, as though the sofa wished to perform surgery on you), the characterless glass desk, the framed art that looked like smudged Xeroxes of stock photos, the whole cheaply built development. A bronzeish pot the size of a toddler stood in the corner, as though punished, and he knew that even the arrangement of branches therein had been purchased at a store. The living room was filled with fake antiques. The sofa was distressed. So was the table. So (joked Peter Elroy to himself) was Peter Elroy. Truthfully, he was so delighted at the badness of the taste that he could ignore the shame of that delight, and the wisp of sorrow that none of his long-ago lessons had stuck.

Of course there were the film posters in the den, each exactly the same size and framed the same way. Four of them, the newest more than ten years old. No poster for the first one: Peter Elroy's star vehicle, the reason he and Ian had not spoken in thirty years.

"Why are you wearing a ring on your little finger?" the boy asked. He stood in the doorway of the den, almond-eyed and brunet, like his young mother. Nothing of his father's swaybacked puffed-chest stance.

"It's a signet ring."

"Men don't wear jewelry," the boy said.

"Don't they? Your father has a wedding ring, surely. Not even his first. Third wife, no doubt third wedding ring. Unless he recycles them. Does he?"

The boy said, "You don't have a wedding ring."

"Wedding rings are a continental affectation. I have the important piece of equipment."

"What?"

"A wife. Original model. Myra."

"What?"

"My wife's named Myra. Where's your sister?"

"Asleep."

"Wake her up, why don't you. Send her in."

After thinking about it, the boy said, "I'm supposed to look out for her."

Peter Elroy laughed. "Fair enough."

"I know everything about mummies," said the boy.

"I don't doubt it. The funerary arts. If I don't last the week, tell your parents I'd like a few dead cats in my tomb. Don't bother about mummification."

"They take the brains out with hooks through the nose."

"I know. Happened to me once."

"No it didn't."

"No, it didn't. I'm joking. Where's your father? Making a movie?"

"What?"

"Don't say what. Say, I beg your pardon."

The boy sat in the wheeled chair at the glass desk and opened its drawer. "He's teaching a master class," he said at last.

"Of course. Not just a *class*. A *master* class. Do you watch his movies?"

The boy shrugged. "I don't get screen time."

"What does that mean?"

"No TV or computers or stuff like that."

"Ah." Peter Elroy leaned back and the sofa tilted. The movement was a knife in his back. He struggled to get himself upright. "No television! No computers! What century is this?"

"I don't know."

"You don't know what century it is?"

"No," said the boy.

"Lucky," said Peter Elroy. He had the sense on the leather sofa of being a dollar bill folded into a wallet. No. Not a dollar bill. A receipt. "What I wouldn't give. I had rather too much screen time, courtesy of your father. That's what happened to *me*. Did you know that?"

"No," said the boy.

"Ask your father. He's a wolf."

The boy thought about this. "He's not."

"I don't mean it badly," Peter Elroy lied. He hadn't meant to bring up the documentary, or wolves, either. "Wolves are marvelous creatures. Do you know about them? They're not small. Everyone imagines them as small. They're this big." He held his hand up over his head. "You must never say anything bad about a wolf."

"Why not?"

"Because they will eat you. Like this." He lunged and barked. "Let's hear you do a wolf."

The boy tried.

"That's a *coyote*," said Peter Elroy in a disgusted voice. "Wolf. Listen."

He'd been dreaming of wolves lately; he had wolves on the brain. In his dreams he couldn't tell whether they'd come to protect him or rip him to shreds, and though he thought about telling Myra, he was worried she would say, *Well, it's obvious. Wolf equals death.* She prided herself these days on how easily she could say *death* and *dying,* and Peter Elroy was mostly grateful for that ease.

No, he thought now. The wolf wasn't death.

"Try again," he said to the boy, but then the Young Mother poked her head into the den and said, "Could there be less howling, please?"

On her hip she balanced the little girl, who had a look of Victorian disapproval on her face. Even the girl's dark hair looked annoyed and half-awake.

"Let's go make lunch," the Young Mother said to her.

"I don't vant to. I vant to stay my Desi."

"I'll keep an eye on her," said the boy.

The Young Mother looked at Peter Elroy. "Please," he said, and meant it. Three-year-olds were worse at conversation than five-year-olds, but on the other hand they were better people. They lacked ambition. He sensed that the boy already believed himself to be the smartest person in any room.

"Down you go," the Young Mother said to the girl, and set her on the floor. "Can I get you anything, Peter?"

"Glass of cold arsenic."

"We're out."

"A glass of white wine, then."

She looked at her watch. "Really?"

"Palliative," he explained. He turned to the girl. "Can *you* do a wolf?"

"All right," the Young Mother said dubiously, and left the room.

"*Rawer!*" said the girl, showing her little pointed incisors.

"Very good," said Peter Elroy. "Extremely frightening."

"Jane thinks she's not going to die," the boy offered.

Peter Elroy appraised her. "If anyone could buck the system, it'll be Jane here."

"But everybody dies!" the boy said, exasperated. "That's how it *works*."

"*Rawer!*" the girl said again.

"No, Jane. Like this." The boy howled from his stomach. It was a good performance. "I'm not afraid of wolves," he said when he was done.

"That's not interesting," Peter Elroy said. "Let's talk about what you *are* afraid of. Mummies?"

"I'm not afraid of anything," said the boy.

"Ghosts, then."

"I'm not afraid of ghosts. I'm not afraid of pirates. I'm not afraid of lions."

"I'm not afraid lions," said the little girl.

"Shh, Jane. I'm not afraid of vampires."

"I'm afraid vampires," the girl said sadly.

"Me, too," said Peter Elroy.

"I'm afraid volves," said the little girl.

"I'm kind of afraid of bullies," said the boy.

"I was a bully," said Peter Elroy. "A man needs to be a bully, if he wants to get anything done. Your father will tell you otherwise, I imagine, but do you know what? Your father is a bully. Bigger bully than me."

The boy frowned, his eyebrows serious. "My dad is *not* a bully."

"He bullied me pretty bad. One day you'll watch that movie and see. There's nothing like a wolf, you know. A volf. Your father," he said, and then he stopped. He told himself it was the morphine that was making him talk to small children like this, but he would have any day of his life: he just spent no time with children. "You must look after your parents, you know. Otherwise the wolves will eat you."

"Will they really?" said the boy.

"Not out of *meanness*. It's just their nature."

The boy scratched his chin in a cartoon of thoughtfulness. "How do you get them not to?"

"You talk to them. Wolves are very reasonable. Do you speak wolf?"

The children shook their heads, but the girl said, "I do, a little bit," and she measured with her index finger and thumb the little bit of wolf she spoke.

"No, you don't," said the boy.

"It's all right," said Peter Elroy, "I'm fluent."

Eventually the Young Mother cleared the children out for lunch. She put the glass of wine on the desk, where he couldn't reach it. "You rest," she said to Peter Elroy. "That sofa reclines, if you're interested."

She had not mentioned his diagnosis, and he knew that she wouldn't. This was the trouble with a terminal illness: you weren't allowed to be sick, you were only dying, and nobody wanted the answer to the question *How are you feeling?* to be *Ever closer to death, thanks.*

Once she'd gone, he sat back carefully, so as not to call any of the sofa's hardware into action. For a moment he imagined making a break for it while the children ate their lunch. He would step through the sliding glass doors and just—*go*. He could picture them opening the door to the den, warily at first (so as not to disturb him), then flinging it open, then looking around in shock. The strange gentleman was gone. Perhaps he'd leave his cuff links and ring behind, perhaps nothing but a cutting scent that might be either an expensive cologne or a cheap antiseptic. They'd touch the leather of the sofa where he'd been sitting. *It's still warm. He can't have gotten far.*

The truth was he wasn't sure he could stand up off the sofa. Instead he looked at the woods, not filled with wolves but dotted with chipmunks. The trees were so slender you could see the passing traffic on their far side.

Peter Elroy, disappear? He had no talent for it. That was the problem.

Unlike Ian, whose name was at the bottom of those four posters (where *was* Peter's?) but who wasn't in evidence anywhere else in this awful, characterless house—and hadn't Peter tried to teach Ian that character was everything? Even the children seemed to belong only to the wife, lean and dark, whatever her family background was: she was some ethnic cocktail he couldn't pinpoint, and that irked him, he wanted to ask her what she was, but you weren't allowed to do that anymore.

Ian Casey, the invisible man. That was what he was famous for, how he made his living: he edited out even his shadow if it fell across an interviewee, his most passing camera-shouldering reflection in a shop window. Peter could only imagine what he looked like now: heavier, the sandy blond hair grown long and sandy gray. *Reclusive director Ian Casey,* he was occasionally called, as though he lived in a folly at the back of someone's garden instead of in an ugly gated community. The people in his films seemed to forget that he was there, that the microphone was live and the film was rolling. They said things they never should have, and they said them at length. He gave them enough rope. He'd given Peter Elroy enough, thirty years before. He'd said, "A story about an unlikely friendship. You and me. Just talking."

So they borrowed a car and drove cross-country. Or rather, Peter drove. Ian didn't know how, and besides, someone had to hold the camera. It was 1981. They'd known each other since they'd been teenagers and they'd always talked about a cross-country trip. Ian was in grad school in New York; Peter had finished his second year teaching economics to undergraduates in New Hampshire. Ian was small and fair-haired, in dirty T-shirts from fifteen years before, Dylan and the Dead. Peter favored ragtime and off-color antique jazz you couldn't play on the radio. He pomaded his dark hair and wore cuff links and mocked.

Big Peter, little Ian. Those last days of his illusions. If they were illusions. He still didn't know whether the film had caused his downfall or simply pointed out that the downfall was inevitable.

He mocked Iowans and he mocked Mississippians. In Nevada he wanted to visit a brothel so he could mock both the prostitutes and their customers. He patted waitresses on their behinds as they walked past—that was part of the joke. He was a young man who acted like a daft rich uncle from a 1930s movie. He sang along to the dirty songs on the tape deck. He joked. He was *funny*. Ask anyone! Ask Ian Casey, who—Peter Elroy was sure of this—scrubbed the soundtrack clean of his own laughter at Peter's jokes.

Even when Ian showed him the movie—screened on a sheet in his New York apartment, the spring after the trip—Peter didn't get it. Surprised, yes, to see that Ian had edited himself out of every frame, that he'd turned a conversation into a monologue. But he still thought it was good, he believed (as he'd believed for some time) that he would become the most famous economist in America. Talk shows, news hours, op-ed pages. The movie would get him there faster, and when he watched it he saw himself saying wonderful, shocking things.

Later, he tried not to be too hard on himself for not understanding. There wasn't a man in the world smart enough to see his own subtext.

In the forest, the wind and the wolves both howled: it was a competition. *The minute we are born, we are on our way to death,* a visiting hospital chaplain had once told Peter Elroy, but that was bullshit, wasn't it. You might as well claim that you are on your way to sleep from the moment you wake up, true enough for a few people but not for most. The path to death was less definite than that, and Peter Elroy had just started to look for it and couldn't find it, couldn't find it, forgot what he was looking for. He had the sense that he was batting branches out of his way. Something was coming for him and he had to escape.

He woke up with a hand on his forehead.

"Peter—"

As he'd napped the sofa had slowly reclined of its own accord. He blinked up at the ceiling, and then at the Young Mother, who leaned over him.

"Can I get you anything?" she asked.

His skull was still swamped with sleep. The hand wasn't helping, and he struggled underneath it.

"Sorry," she said, and stood up. "You just didn't look comfortable like that."

He nodded.

"Can I get you some dinner?" she said.

"Is it dinnertime?"

"Past," she said. "I just put the kids to bed. Tell me what you'd like to eat."

She didn't know how to do this. He was hungry but he couldn't imagine negotiating a solution.

"It's all right," he said.

"Shall I make up your bed?" the Young Mother asked. What she meant was: arrange the polyester sheets around the slick leather of the sofa.

"That would mean getting up," he said.

"Here," she said. "Let me help you."

She took his elbow. Together they maneuvered him into the desk chair, and he sat down, panting.

"Does it hurt?"

"Only when I don't take my morphine."

"Should you be drinking?"

"Why not?" He set his arms on the glass desk, which

was freezing cold; he was surprised his wrists didn't bind to the surface. "I'm not operating any heavy machinery."

At last she said, "You look good."

This was such a terrible lie he wanted to punch her. "How would you know? We just met."

"Well," she said. "Well, I've seen the film. You look just the same as you did thirty years ago."

"You've seen it." For some reason that hadn't occurred to him.

"Of course. That's how I met Ian. He came to give a talk at my grad program. He showed it."

"Another master class," he said.

"I guess. You know," she said, "he was really sorry not to be here when you arrived. He misses you a lot, I think."

"Well, next time!" said Peter Elroy in a jolly voice.

"He'll be back by dinner tomorrow."

He shook his head. "You know he won't. That boy is on the lam. He's legging it. He's calling hourly to see if the coast is clear."

"No, he's not."

"Don't lie."

"I'm not lying," she said. "He wouldn't do that to me."

"Ah," said Peter Elroy, looking around the room. "All right. No poster, by the way? Here am I, the eponymous Peter Elroy."

She looked at the wall, and then he could see a hole where the nail had been.

"We took it down before you came," she said at last.

He remembered the poster: a picture of him, looking

over his shoulder, a horrible smirk on his face. The name of the film—him again, his name—at the bottom. It played on the festival circuit before PBS picked it up and demolished his life. "That film's older than you," he said.

"About the same."

"What did you think?"

"Of *Peter Elroy*? It's been ages. I don't really remember it."

"Me neither," he said, though that wasn't true. He'd only seen it once but he thought he could describe every frame. For a while after the broadcast he thought about watching it again, to see what he'd missed, but that seemed an exercise in self-loathing.

"Anyhow, you're different now," the Young Mother said.

"I am *not*," he said hotly. "I never was that way in the first place."

"You said those things. Nobody made you."

Those things. He'd said them for years to no ill effect, those things, things that made people gasp and yell and fume and laugh. Things that made his students that year argue back or nod in agreement and write on their evaluations, *Professor Elroy is a genius* or *He's kind of a jerk but he does know everything about economics.*

But that's how it works, isn't it. Only in person can you be larger than life. On a television screen you're cropped, alone: a buffoon. Once they showed the movie on PBS he became famous (among people who watched PBS, at any rate) as the embodiment of everything that was bad about people who liked money in the early 1980s. He seemed to be a young man who drove across the United States expressly to feel superior to all of its inhabitants, delighted that he had a way to beam his vileness into living rooms everywhere. He didn't get tenure, left his teaching job. He ended up teaching in junior colleges awhile, and then got a job with the Small Business Association, giving extremely cautious advice.

"I can see where you didn't realize how you'd come off. That's the thing about privilege," the Young Mother explained.

"Oh, fucking *privilege*," he said.

"When you come from money—"

"Who says I come from money? Surely your husband didn't tell you that. His lies are generally ones of omission."

He could see her take him in, the cuff links, the expensive shirt that had been starched—actually starched! in the twenty-first century!—the hair that he still combed back. Everything about him suggested generations of money. That was on purpose.

"Well," she said, "you did. In the film. Didn't you?"

"Maybe I come from Dorchester," he said. "Maybe the Caseys were rich in comparison to my family. Maybe I knew his mother and kissed his kid sister. In the old days you were supposed to be *ashamed* of coming from nothing. Now it's the opposite. Nothing is worse than childhood comfort, if you want to really make it. Ah!" he said. "I can see you're already more interested in me. All my mitigating circumstances. You can forgive me if I came from nothing."

"But did you?"

"Did I what?"

"Come from nothing!"

"You're not *listening*," he said. But he couldn't say it. Only Ian knew Peter Elroy before he was Peter Elroy, when he was Pete O'Neill from Dorchester (the first thing he learned to do in college was pronounce *Dorchester* like someone not from Dorchester; a linguistics professor had explained that the first vowel sound was a giveaway, Dwachester, nearly).

"Look," he pleaded. "You live with a documentarian. Surely you understand that everything is a matter of editing. I'm sorry. He's not here. Did I say all those things? Yes. I was answering questions that your future husband asked me."

"You're tired," she said, and at first he was insulted and then he realized she spent her day telling unreasonable people they were tired and then he realized it was true. He was tired.

"I'll make your bed up," she said.

With his thumb he felt his signet ring, bought from his favorite antiques dealer in Portland, Maine, when he was a freshman, visible in the film. Even, if he remembered correctly, in the poster. He wondered for the first time whether it might have made a difference if the film had been honest about his origins. But he never would have been honest. He could be seen as a poor kid, or a fraud, or an asshole. Nobody felt pity for an asshole, so that's what he chose. He hated pity, though now it was the medium he lived in, a kind of emotional aspic he was too weak to punch aside.

The Young Mother was leaning over the sofa, and he had an urge to pat her bottom.

"He's probably screening *Peter Elroy* tonight," she said over her shoulder. "It's the one colleges request, you know."

She stood up suddenly and he put his hand on her torso, higher up than he'd intended. He could feel the weight of her breast in the crook of his thumb, the underwire of her brassiere just below.

She looked at him sorrowfully. "Privilege doesn't just mean money, you know."

"He assassinated me," Peter Elroy said at last. "I loved him anyhow."

In Las Vegas all those years before, they found an old boxing gym. They'd met in a boxing ring, after all, at the Boys' Club.

"It feels good to hit someone in the face," said Peter Elroy to the camera after the match. He was laughing, absurd in his slicked-back hair, his trunks pulled up above his waist. "It feels *great*. Especially a guy who won't fight back. That's where the real pleasure is. When you hit and hit and the guy just gives you the big girlish eyes, *stop it, you brute*!"

He was talking to Ian, of course. He was speaking of himself. Ian, who had just hit Peter in the face. Peter, who would not fight back: he was too squeamish, too afraid he might do real damage, he could look into the future and see that he'd never forgive himself if he broke Ian's nose. When they were fifteen, he'd promised Mrs. Casey he'd look after Ian, and he was scared of nearly nobody but Dolly Casey.

"My God," said Peter to the camera, afterwards, the pain in his jaw just starting to assert itself. "It does feel good."

Doesn't it? You got me, Ian.

Nobody made you say those things, the Young Mother had said, but that wasn't true. Everyone did, all the time. They begged him to say those things. Especially Ian, because they were what he thought. Ian was shy. Peter put everything into words.

That movie was supposed to be a love story: the little quiet guy and the big loud guy who had known each other forever, who insulted each other, who got along because they both suspected the other might be—*might be*—his intellectual equal, when the rest of the world were morons.

It could have been a love story. Now, thirty years later, thirty years since he'd seen it, Peter Elroy decided to believe that it was. He'd discovered, as he got sicker, that he could do that, resolve to believe something, and he didn't know if it was a side effect of cancer or medication or the closeness of death or even age—he would die prematurely but he wasn't young, not an age that was precocious for anything but death. An age to *tsk* over, that was all.

It *was* meant as a love letter. Peter Elroy had thought so when he saw it, and Ian Casey had, too. It was the rest of the world who got it wrong.

The Young Mother left without helping him back to the sofa, which he could tell would be impossible to sleep on anyhow: the sheets would slip, whisper awfully in his ear. In a moment he would use the wheels of the desk chair to propel himself to the bathroom down the hall. He tried to look past the reflection of the room in the sliding glass doors. Of course Ian wouldn't come. He had to stop hoping he would. Myra would collect him, would sit and talk a while with the Young Mother, would say, "It was worth a try," would say, as they drove away, "At least you met his family." The wine was still on the desk and now he could reach. He drank, wincing at the warmth of it. He could practically taste the picture of the adorable animal on the label. Six-dollar wine. Wine for people who either don't drink wine or drink too much of it.

He felt the cell phone in his shirt pocket and wished Myra would call.

They'd been married twenty-five years and he could still feel a panic—not in his heart, just below—any time he suspected she wasn't thinking about him. It laid him as low as any deeper, more sustained unrequited love he'd ever felt. Of course she loved him, he knew that, he just wanted her to love him *all the time*.

He tried to send her a message on brain waves. *Whatever you were thinking of: think of me.* Another thing technology had ruined, the ability to dial a number, let it ring, hang up. How often had he done that, only wanting to change what a girl was thinking, without her knowing he was the one who'd done it.

At that very moment, he thought, the lights were coming up, students were applauding, and the film professor who'd organized the event was saying, "Mr. Casey was kind enough to agree to a short Q & A." A young man with a Q puts his hand in the air. No. A young woman. "Yes," Ian says, and she says, "How did you *find* that guy?"

Say my name, thought Peter Elroy, first at the girl, and then at Ian. But his imagination failed, and he couldn't think what Ian might answer.

He felt his phone again. If only he could picture where Myra was. They'd be back at Evie's house (a place he'd never seen) surrounded by Evie's children and grandchildren (people he'd never met).

Somewhere, a dog barked. No, it didn't. Only in novels did you catch such a break, a hollow in your stomach answered by some far-off dog making an unanswered dog-call. Dogs were not allowed at Drake's Landing. Still, surely, somewhere in the world a dog *was* barking, a cat was hissing, a parrot with an unkind recently deceased owner was saying something inappropriate to an animal shelter volunteer.

Outside, in the light from the Drake's Landing's floodlights, the snow sparkled like something that wasn't snow. Diamonds, or asphalt, or emery boards.

A knock at the door: the children.

"Shouldn't you be in bed?" Peter Elroy asked. He pointed at the hallway behind them and frowned, though he knew he was less frightening now that it was dark and his glasses were just clear glass.

"We had a bad dream," said the boy.

"About the volf," said the girl.

He did not feel repentant. All he ever wanted: people thinking of him against their will. What got him in trouble in the first place.

"Are wolves real?" the boy asked, in a voice that knew the answer.

They had not come to him for comfort: they would have woken the Young Mother for that. She would have told them that there were no wolves in Connecticut. Or she would have lied entirely, said, no, wolves were not real, not anymore, they belonged with ancient Egypt and dinosaurs and Knights of the Realm and pirates of the Long John Silver sort, in books and legend, the glittering viciousness children loved, sabers, fangs, cutlasses, claws: things they could claim for themselves because the original owners were extinct.

"Of course they're real," Peter Elroy said. "And they're coming. Not for you. They wouldn't eat you. You're too small. Too thin. All bone. A wolf would look at you and think, *Disgusting*."

"Dis-custing," the girl echoed.

"But I'm lovely," said Peter Elroy. "I'm delicious."

"We'll protect you," said the boy.

"Darling," said Peter Elroy, "it's all right. Let them come."

And they did, one night soon afterwards.

Thunderstruck

1.

Wes and Laura had not even known Helen was missing when the police brought her home at midnight. Her long bare legs were marbled red with cold, and she had tear tracks on her face, but otherwise she looked like her ordinary placid awkward middle-school self: snarled hair, chapped lips, pink cheeks. She'd lost her pants somewhere, and she held in one fist a seemingly empty plastic garbage bag, brown, the yellow drawstring pulled tight at its neck. Laura thought the policemen should have given her something to cover up. Though what did cops know about clothing: maybe they thought that long black T-shirt was a dress. It had a picture of a pasty overweight man in swashbuckler's clothes captioned, in movie marquee letters, LINDA.

"She's twelve!" Wes told the police, as though they were

the ones who'd lured the girl from her bed. "She's only *twelve*."

"Sorry, Daddy," Helen said.

Laura grabbed her daughter by the wrist and pulled her in before the police could change their minds and arrest her, or them. She took the garbage bag from Helen, un-cinched the aperture, and stared in, looking for evidence, missing clothing, wrong-doers.

"Nitrous oxide party," said the taller officer, who looked like all the Irish boys Laura had grown up with. Maybe he was one. "They inhale from those bags. The owner of the house is in custody. Some kid had a bad reaction, she threw them all onto the lawn. The others scattered but your daughter stayed with the boy in distress. So there's that."

"There's that," said Wes.

Helen gave her mother a sweet, sinuous, beneath-the-arm hug. She'd gotten so tall she had to stoop to do it; she was Laura's height now. "Mommy, I love you," she said. She was a theatrical child. She always had been.

"You could have suffocated!" Laura said, throttling the bag.

"I didn't put it over my head," said Helen.

Laura ripped a hole in the bottom of the bag, as though that were still a danger.

This was her flaw as a parent, she thought later: she had never truly gotten rid of a single maternal worry. They were all in the closet, with the minuscule footed pajamas and hand-knit baby hats, and every day Laura took them out, unfolded them, tried to put them to use. Kit was seven, Helen nearly a teenager, and a small, choke-worthy item on the floor still dropped Laura, scrambling, to her knees. She could not bear to see her girls on their bicycles, both the cycling and the cycling *away*. Would they even remember her cell-phone number, if they and their phones were lost separately? Did anyone memorize numbers anymore? The electrical outlets were still dammed with plastic, in case someone got a notion to jab at one with a fork.

She had never worried about breathing intoxicating gas from Hefty bags. Another worry. Put it on the pile. Soon it might seem quaint, too.

She blamed her fretting on Helen's first pediatrician, who had told her there was no reason to obsess about Sudden Infant Death Syndrome. "It'll happen or it won't," said Dr. Moody. Laura had found this an unacceptable philosophy. Her worry for the baby had heat and energy: how could it be useless? Nobody had warned her how deeply babies slept, how you couldn't always see them breathing. You watched, and watched, you touched their dozy stomachs to feel their clockwork. Even once the infant Helen started sleeping through the night, Laura checked on her every two hours. Sometimes at two A.M. she was so certain that Helen had died, she felt an electric shock to the heart, and this (she believed) started Helen's heart, too: her worry was the current that kept them both alive. Kit, too, when Kit, a surprise, crashed sweetly into their lives.

Maybe that was what happened to Helen. She was supposed to be an only child. She'd been promised. Kit was a flirtatious baby, a funny self-assured toddler. She made people laugh. Poor awkward honking Helen: it would be hard to be Kit's older sister. Growing up, Laura had hated the way her parents had compared her to her brother—Ben was good at math, so there was no point in her trying; Laura was more outgoing, so she had to introduce her brother to friends—but once she had her own children she understood comparison was necessary. It was how you discovered their personalities: the light of one child threw the other child into relief, no different from how she, at thirteen, had known what she looked like only by comparing the length of her legs and the color of her hair to her friends and their legs and their hair.

Helen hit her sister; Helen was shut in her room; afterwards all four of them would go to the old-fashioned ice cream parlor with the twisted wire chairs. She and Wes couldn't decide when to punish and when to indulge, when a child was testing the boundaries and needed discipline, and when she was demanding, in the brutish way of children, more love. In this way, their life had been pasted together with marshmallow topping and hot fudge. Shut her in her room. Buy her a banana split. Do both: see where it gets you.

Helen sneaking out at night. Helen doing drugs.

Children were unfathomable. The same thing that could stop them from breathing in the night could stop them from loving you during the day. Could cause them to be brought home by the police without their pants or a good explanation.

That long night Laura and Wes interrogated her. Laura, mostly, while Wes examined the corners of Helen's bedroom and looked griefstruck. Whose house? Laura asked. What had she been doing there? What about Addie, her best friend, Addie of the braces and the clarinet? Was she there? Laura wanted to know everything. No, that wasn't true. She wanted to know nothing, she wanted to be told there was nothing to worry about: she wanted from Helen only consolation. She knew she couldn't yell comfort out of her but she didn't know what else to do. "What were you *thinking*?" she asked Helen, too loudly, as though it were thinking that was dangerous.

Helen shrugged. Then she pulled aside the neck of the T-shirt to examine her own shoulder and shrugged again. Over the bed was a poster that matched her T-shirt: the same guy, light caught in the creases of his leather pants, pale lipstick, dark eyeliner.

"What happened to your nose?" Laura asked.

Helen covered it with her hand. "Someone tried to pierce it."

"Helen! You do not have permission."

Wes said, looking at the poster, "Linda sure is pretty."

"*He's* not Linda," said Helen. "Linda's the *band*."

Laura sat down next to her. Helen's nose was red, nicked, but whoever had wielded the needle had given up. "Beautiful Helen, why would you?" Laura said. Helen bit her lip to avoid smiling straight out. Then she looked up at the poster.

"He must be hot in those pants," Wes said.

"Probably," said Helen. She slid under her bedclothes and touched her nose again. "I'm tired, I think."

"Poor Linda," said Wes. He rubbed his face in what looked like disbelief. "To suffer so for his art."

. . .

"We'll go to Paris," Wes told Laura. It was four A.M.

"Yes." They were exhausted, unslept. Helen seemed like an intelligence test they were failing, had been failing for years. Better to flee. Paris. "Why?" she said.

"Helen's always wanted to go."

"She has?"

"All those children's books. *Madeline*. Some Richard Scarry mouse, I think. Babar. Kit's old enough to enjoy it now. We'll—we'll get Helen painting lessons. Kit, too, if she's interested. Or I'll take them to museums and we'll draw. Eat pastries. Get *out* of here. Your brother's always offering us booty from his frequent-flier millions. Let's say *yes*. Let's go."

The biggest ice cream sundae in the world. Wes taught printmaking at a community college and had the summer off. Laura worked for a caterer and was paid only by the job. They'd have to do it frugally but they could swing it.

"All right," said Laura. They stayed up till morning, looking at apartments on the Internet. By seven A.M. Ben had e-mailed back that he was happy to give them the miles; by eight they had booked the flights. They arranged for one of Wes's students to look after the house and the dog for the five weeks they'd be gone. It was astonishing how quickly the trip came together.

The plan was to disrupt their lives, a jolt to Helen's system before school started again in the fall. The city would be strange and beautiful, as Helen herself was strange and beautiful. Perhaps they'd understand her there. Perhaps the problem all this time was that her soul had been written in French.

They flew overnight from Boston; they hadn't been on a plane since before Kit was born. Inside the terminal they tried to lead the family suitcases, old plaid things with insufficient silver wheels along the keels, prone to tipping. Honeymoon luggage from the last century: that was how long it had been since they'd traveled. At Charles de Gaulle, all of the Europeans pulled behind them like obedient dogs their long-handled perfectly balanced bags and they murmured into their cell phones. Laura patted her pocket, felt the switched-off phone that she'd been assured would cost too much to use here, and felt sorry for it. Her suitcase fell over like a shot dog. Only Helen seemed to understand how to walk through the airport, as though it were a sport suited to the pubescent female body, a long-legged stride that made the suitcase heel.

Outside the morning was hot, and French, and blinding, and Wes was already loading the cases into the trunk of a taxi with the grim care of a man disposing of corpses. Laura thought: *What a bad idea this was*. She squeezed into the back of the cab between the girls, another old caution: proximity sometimes made them pinch each other. She had to fold her torso along the spine like the covers of a book. Wes got into the passenger seat and unraveled the piece of paper with the address of the apartment they'd rented over the Internet.

"*Excusez-moi,*" Wes said to the driver. "*Je parle français très mal.*" The cab driver nodded impatiently. Yes, very badly, it was the most self-evident sentence ever spoken: anything Wes might have said in French would have conveyed the same information. The driver took the scrap from Wes's hand.

"*L'appartement,*" said Helen, "*se trouve dans le troisième arrondissement, je crois, monsieur. Cent vingt-deux rue du Temple.*"

At this the driver smiled. "*Ah! Bon! Merci, mademoiselle. Le troisième, exactement.*"

They were so smashed into the back Laura couldn't turn to look at Helen. "You speak French!" she said, astounded.

"I *take* French, Mommy. You know that. I don't *speak* it."

"You're fluent!" said Laura.

The street was crooked, and the taxi driver bumped onto the sidewalk to let them get out. In English he said, "Welcome here." Across the street were a few wholesale jewelry and pocketbook stores, and Laura was stunned by how cheap the merchandise hanging in the window looked, and she wondered whether they'd managed to book an apartment in the only tacky quarter of Paris. The door to their building was propped open. The girls moaned as they walked up the stairs, dragging their bags. "I thought it was on the *fourth* floor," said Helen, and Wes said, "They count floors differently here."

"Like a different alphabet?" said Kit.

The staircase narrowed the further up they went, as though a trick of perspective. At the top were two doors.

One had an old-fashioned business card taped to it. *M. Petit.* That was their contact. Wes knocked, and a small elderly man in an immaculate white shirt and blue tie answered.

"*Bonjour!*" he said. He came out and led them to the other door. He held on to the tie, as though he wanted to make sure they saw it. "*Bienvenu, venez ici. Ici, ici, madame, monsieur, mademoiselles.*"

"*Je parle français très mal,*" said Wes, and there was that look again. M. Petit dropped his tie.

"You do it, Helen," said Laura.

"*Bonjour, monsieur,*" said Helen, and he brought them around the apartment and described everything, pantomiming and saying, "*Vous comprenez?*" and Helen answered in a nasal, casual, quacking way, "*Ouais. Ouais. Ouais.*"

"What did he say?" Wes asked when M. Petit had gone.

"Something about hot water," she said. "Something about garbage. We need to get calling cards for the phone. He lives next door if we need anything."

"Something about garbage," said Kit. "Real helpful."

The apartment was tiny but high-ceilinged, delightful, seemingly carved from gingerbread: a happy omen for their trip, Laura decided. The girls would sleep in twin beds in one room, Wes and Laura across the hall in a bed that was nearly double but not quite. A three-quarters double bed, like the three-quarters cello that Helen played. The windows looked out on next-door chimney pots. The living room was the size of its oriental rug. The kitchen included a sink, a two-burner hot plate, a waist-high fridge, and a tabletop oven. It was the oldest building any of them had ever stood in.

"Why are the pillows square?" Kit asked.

"They just *are*," said Helen knowingly. She leaned her head out the little window. *Five stories up and no way to shimmy down,* thought Laura. Helen said, "I want to stay here forever."

"We'll see," said Wes. "Come on. Let's go. Let's see Paris."

Jet lag and sunshine turned the city hallucinogenically beautiful. "We'll keep going," said Wes. "Till bedtime. Best way to deal with jet lag." Down the rue des Francs Bourgeois, through the Place des Vosges over to the Bastille, along the river, across one bridge, and another: then they stood staring at Notre Dame's back end, all its flying buttresses kicking at Laura's sternum.

"Notre Dame is *here*?" said Helen. An insinuating wind tugged at the bottom of her shirt; she held it down.

"In Paris, yes," said Wes.

"But we just *walked* to it?"

Wes laughed. "We can walk everywhere."

They kept walking, looking for the right café, feeling the heat like optimism on their limbs. Laura swore Helen's French got even better as the day went on: she translated the menu at the café, she asked for directions, she found the right amount of money to pay for midafternoon crepes. She negotiated the purchase of two primitive prepaid cell phones, one for Wes and one for Laura. At home the girls had phones, but in Paris they would always be with one of their parents.

What was that odd blooming in Laura's torso? A sense that this was how it happened: you became dependent on your children, and it was all right.

They kept moving in order to stay awake until it was sort of bedtime. At six Laura thought she could feel the sidewalk tilting up like a Murphy bed, and they went to the tiny grocery store behind their building, got bread and meat and wine, and held up the line first when they didn't understand they needed to pack their own groceries, and again when they couldn't open the slippery plastic bags. Once they were out, they felt triumphant anyhow. Wes raised the baguette like a sword.

They turned down their little street. Up ahead of them a heavyset woman hurried in the middle of the road with a funny hitch, then suddenly turned, worked a shiny black girdle to mid-thigh, and peed in the gutter, an astounding flood that stopped the Langfords.

Helen said, "Awesome."

"That," said Kit, "was impressive."

"City of lights," said Wes.

In their medieval apartment, they ate like medieval people, tearing bread with their teeth, spreading butter with their fingers. They all went to bed at the same time, the girls in their nightgowns—Kit's patterned with roses, Helen's another Linda XXL T-shirt. "Good night, good night," said Laura, standing between their beds. They had never shared a room, her girls. Then she and Wes went across the hall to the other room.

The necessary closeness of the three-quarters bed amplified everything. Her tenderness for Wes, who had been so sure this was the right thing; her worries about how much money this trip would cost; her anxiety at having to use her threadbare high school French. She understood this was the reason she was thirty-six and had never been to Europe. It was a kind of stage fright.

In the morning they discovered that the interior walls were so thin they could hear, just behind the headboard, the noise of M. Petit emptying his bladder as clearly as if he'd been in the same room. It was a long story, the emptying of M. Petit's bladder, with many digressions and false endings.

"We're in Paris," whispered Wes.

"I thought there would be more foie gras and less pee," Laura whispered back.

"Both," said Wes. "There will be plenty of both."

In Paris, Helen became a child again. She was skinny, pubescent, not the lean dangerous blade of a near-teen she'd seemed at home, in skin-tight blue jeans and oversized T-shirts. In Paris you could buy children's shoes and children's clothes for a person who was five-two. The sales were on, clothing so cheap they kept buying. Helen chose candy-colored skirts, and T-shirts with cartoon characters.

At le boulevard Richard-Lenoir, near the Bastille, Helen bought a vinyl purse with a long strap, in which she kept a few euros, a ChapStick, her name and address, a notebook for writing down her favorite sights. She walked hand in hand with Kit: they were suddenly friends, as though their fighting had been an allergic reaction to American air. Both girls picked up French as though by static electricity, and they spoke it to each other, tossing their hair over their shoulders. *"Ouais,"* they said, in the way that even Laura, whose brain seemed utterly French-resistant, now recognized as how Parisians quackingly agreed.

There were so many *pâtisseries* and *boulangeries* and *fromageries* that they rated the pain au chocolat of one block against the pain au chocolat of the next. The candy shops were like jewelry stores, the windows filled with twenty-four-carat bonbons. The caterer Laura worked for had given her money to smuggle back some young raw milk cheeses that were illegal in the United States, and Laura decided to taste every *Reblochon* in the city, every *Sainte-Maure de Touraine,* so that on the last day she could buy the best and have them vacuum-packed against the noses of what she liked to imagine were the U.S. Customs Cheese Beagles.

Paris was exactly what she had expected and nothing like it. The mullioned passages full of stamp shops and dollhouse-furniture stores, the expensive wax museum the girls wanted to go back and back to despite not recognizing most of the counterfeit celebrities, the hot-chocolate emporia and the bare-breasted bus-stop ads. These were things she had not known were in Paris but felt she should have. The fast-food joint called Flunch, the Jewish district with its falafel ("Shall we have f'laffel for flunch," Wes said nearly every day). She never really got her bearings in the city, no matter how she studied the map. Paris on paper always looked like a box of peanut brittle that had been dropped onto the ground, the Seine the unraveled ribbon that had held it together.

"What's your favorite thing in Paris?" Wes asked.

"My family," she answered. That was the truth.

After a while they bought a third pay-as-you-go phone for Helen and Kit to share, so the girls could go out in the city together after lunch. Then Wes and Laura would go back to the apartment. She thought every languishing marriage should be prescribed a three-quarter bed. They didn't even think to worry about M. Petit on the other side of the wall until later, when news of his careful, decorous life floated back to them: a ringing phone, a whistling teakettle, a dainty plastic clatter that could only be a dropped button. This was why it was good to be temporary, and for the neighbors to be French.

"How did you know?" Laura asked Wes.

"What do you mean?" he said.

"Helen. How *good* she'd be here."

"I don't know. I just—I felt it. She is, though, isn't she? Good. Sweet. Back to her old self."

Her old self? Laura thought. Helen had never been like this a day in her life.

Still it was a miracle: take the clumsy, eager-to-please girl to Paris. Watch her develop *panache*.

Then it was August. It was hot in Paris. They hadn't realized how hot it would be, and how—Laura thought sometimes—how dirty. The heat conjured up dirt, centuries of cobblestone-caught filth. It was as though Paris had never actually been clean, as though you could smell every drop of blood and piss and shit spilled in the streets since before the days of the revolution. Half the stores and restaurants shut for the month, as the sensible Parisians fled for the coast. French food felt tyrannical. When they chose the wrong place to eat, a café that looked good but where the skin of the confit de canard was flabby and soft, the bread damp, it didn't feel like bad luck: it felt as though they'd fallen for a con. As though the place had hidden the better food in the back, for the actually French.

Laura was ready to go home. August was like a page turning. July had felt lucky: August, cursed. From the first day, Laura would think later, no mistake.

The day of Helen's accident—or perhaps the day before; they would never know exactly when the accident happened—she was as lovely and childish as ever. In the makeup section of the Monoprix, she lipsticked a mouth on the edge of her hand, the lower lip on her thumb and the upper on her index finger.

"*Bonjour,*" she said to her mother, through her hand.

"*Bonjour, madame,*" said Laura, who did not like speaking French even under these circumstances. The Monoprix was air-conditioned. They spent a lot of time there.

France had refined the features of Helen's face—Laura had always thought of them as slightly coarse, the thick chap-prone lips, the too-bright eyes—the face, Laura thought now, of a girl who would do anything for a boy, even a boy who didn't care. Her own face, once upon a time. But in Paris, Helen had changed. She had lost the eagerness, the oddness, the blunt difficulty of her features. She had become a Parisienne. Laura tucked the label of Helen's shirt in, felt the warmth of her back, and with the force of previously unseen heartache she knew: they would fly back in three days and nothing, nothing would have changed. They would step back into the aftermath of all they hadn't dealt with.

"Are you looking forward to going home?" Laura asked.

Helen pouted. Then she jutted her thumb out, made her bee-stung hand pout, too. "*Non,*" she said. "*J'adore Paris.* I'd like to stay here forever."

"Not me," said Kit. "I miss Frogbert."

"Who?" said Helen.

"Our *dog,*" said Kit. "Oh, very funny."

"Forever," Helen said again. "Daddy!" she called across to her father, who was just walking into the store with an antique lampshade. He wanted to stay in France forever, too. Laura could imagine him using the lampshade as an excuse: *How can we get this on the plane? We'd better just stay here.*

"Look!" he said. "Hand-painted. Sea serpents."

And they were, a chain of lumpy, dimwitted sea serpents linked mouth to tail around the hem of the shade. It was a grimy, preposterous thing in the gleaming cosmetic aisle of Monoprix.

Helen took it with the flats of her palms. "It's awesome," she said. "Daddy, it's perfect."

Laura did not think she had ever seen that look on Helen's face—not just happiness, but the wish to convey that happiness to someone else, a generosity. That was the expression Laura tried to remember later, to paste down in her head, because soon it was gone forever, replaced with a parody of a smile, a look that was not dreamy but dumbstruck, recognizable, not Cinderella asked to the ball, but a stepsister, years later, finally invited back to the palace, forgiven. Because twelve hours later, Wes and Laura, asleep in their antique bed, heard a familiar, forgotten noise: Wes's American cell phone, ringing in the dresser drawer. Why was it on? Laura answered it.

"Have you a daughter?" said the voice on the other end.

The voice belonged to a nurse from the American Hospital of Paris, who said that a young girl had been brought in with a head injury.

"She have a shirt that say *Linda*," said the nurse. "She fell and striked her head."

Laura went to the girls' room, the phone pressed to her ear. Kit was asleep among the square pillows and the overstuffed duvet. Her hair was sweat damp. Helen's bed was empty. Laura looked to the window, as though it was from there she'd fallen, the pavement below upon which she'd struck her head. It was locked into place, ajar to let the air in but fixed. If Helen had left the apartment it would have been the ordinary way.

"*Je ne comprends pas*," Laura said, though the nurse was speaking English.

"She need someone here," said the nurse. "It's bad."

2.

This was why you had two children. This is why you didn't. Wes stood outside their old, old, unfathomably old building. There were no taxis out and he couldn't imagine how to call one. He wondered whether he'd wanted to come to Paris because of the language: the way he'd felt coddled by lack of understanding, delighted to be capable of so little. By now he could get along pretty well, but this question, how Paris worked in the middle of the night, seemed beyond his abilities. Who he needed: Helen, to help him make his way to Helen. The Métro didn't run this late, he knew that much. Upstairs Kit slept on, Laura watching over her, which was why he was alone on the street. She was the spare child. The one who wasn't supposed to be here. The one who was all right. In his panic he had not wanted to go away from her: he'd wanted to crawl into Helen's empty bed, not even caring how warm or cold the sheets were, how long she'd been gone, as though that child were already lost and the only thing to do was watch over the girl who was left.

He GPS'd directions on his smartphone, the American one. Four and a half miles, in a wealthy suburb called Neuilly-sur-Seine. He would walk: he couldn't think of an alternative. If he saw a taxi he would flag it down but the main thing was movement. Westward, as fast as he could, and then he felt he was in a dull, extravagant, incredible movie. He had a quest, and every person he passed seemed hugely important: the man carrying the dozing child, who asked for directions Wes couldn't provide (he hid the phone, he didn't want to stop); the two police carrying riot shields though Wes could not hear any kind of altercation that might require them; the old woman in elegant, filthy cloth-ing who was sweeping out the rhomboid front of a café. All summer he and his women had walked. "It's the only way to understand a city," Wes had said more than once, "we are *flâneurs*." Now he understood that wandering taught you nothing. Only when you moved with purpose could you know a place. Towards someone, away from someone. "Helen," he said aloud, as he walked beneath the Périphé-rique's looping traffic. He had not driven a car in more than a month. They looked like wild animals to him. Everything looked feral, in fact. He wanted a weapon.

It took him more than an hour to get to the upscale western suburb of the American Hospital. By then the sun was rising. He stumbled in, shocked by the lights, the peo-ple. He didn't want to talk to anyone but Helen, he just wanted to find her, but he knew that was impossible so he stopped at the lit-up desk by the door. The sign above it said INFORMATION. Was that INFORMATION in English, or in-formaCEEohn in French?

"*J'arrive,*" he said, as the waiters did in busy restau-rants, though they meant, *I will* and not *I have*. He added, "I walked here."

The man behind the desk had short greasy bangs combed down in points, like a knife edge. "Patient name?"

Wes hesitated. What sort of shape was she in? What in-formation had Laura given the hospital? "Helen Langford." He found some hope inside him: of course Helen was conscious. How else would they have got Wes's American phone number? She wouldn't have remembered the French one.

"ICU," said the man with the serrated hair.

But it turned out that Helen had taken her mother's American phone, had been using it all summer to call first the U.S. and then Paris, to text, to take pictures of herself. When the battery drained, she swapped it for Wes's, recharged, swapped them back. The hospital had found the phone in her pocket, had gone through the contact list and eventually found him.

The ICU doctor was a tall man with heavy black eyebrows and silver sideburns. Wes felt dizzied by his perfect English, his unidentifiable accent, the rush of details. Helen had been dropped off at the front door by some boys. She probably had not been injured in this neighborhood: the boys brought her here, as though *American* were a medical condition that needed to be treated at a specialist hospital. They had done a CAT scan and an MRI. The only injury was to her head. She had fallen upon it. Her blood screened clean for drugs but she'd had a few drinks. "Some sweet wine, maybe, made her clumsy. Hijinks," said the doctor, dropping the initial h. *Ijinks.* Not an Anglophone then. "Children. Stupid."

"Is she dead?" he asked the doctor.

"What? No. She's had a tumble, that's true. She struck her head. Right now, we're keeping her unconscious, we put in a tube." The doctor tapped his graying temple. "To relieve the pressure."

What was causing pressure? "Air?" Wes said.

"Air? Ah, no. Fluid. Building up. So the tube—" The doctor made a sucking noise. "So far it's working. Later today, tomorrow, we will know more."

Wes had expected his daughter to be tiny in the bed, but she looked substantial, womanly. Her eyes were closed. The side of her head was obscured by an enormous bandage, with the little slurping tube running from it. No, not slurping. It didn't make a sound. Wes had imagined that, thanks to the doctor.

Her little room was made of glass walls, blindered by old-fashioned wheeled screens. There was nothing to sit on. For half an hour he crouched by the bed and spoke to her, though her eyes were closed. She was slack. Every part of her.

"Helen," he said, "Helen. You can tell us anything. You should, you know." They'd been the kind of parents who'd wanted to know nothing, or the wrong things. It hit him with the force of a conversion: all along they'd believed what they didn't acknowledge didn't exist. Here, proof: the unsayable existed. "Helen," he said to his sleeping daughter. "I will never be mad at you again. We're starting over. Tell me *anything*."

A fresh start. He erased the photos and texts from the phone: he wanted to know everything in the future, not the past. Later he'd regret it, he'd want names, numbers, the indecipherable slang-ridden texts of French teenagers, but as he scrolled down, deleting, affirming each deletion, it felt like a kind of meditative prayer: *I will change. Life will broaden and better.*

Half an hour later he stepped out to the men's room and found Kit and Laura wandering near the vending machines. Kit had been weeping. *Oh, the darling!* he thought. Then he realized that Laura had been grilling her. She was not a sorrowful little sister. She was a confederate.

"We took a taxi," said Laura miserably.

"Good," said Wes.

"Nobody will tell me anything," said Laura. "The goddamn desk."

"All right," said Wes. "She's—"

"How did she *get* here?" said Laura. "Who dropped her *off*?"

"Nobody knows," said Wes, which was what he'd understood.

"Somebody does!"

"Look," said Wes. Before they went to see Helen, he wanted to explain it to her. What he knew now: they needed to talk about everything. They needed to be interested in their daughters' secrets, not terrified. He sat them down on the molded bolted-together plastic chairs along the walls. He was glad for the rest. "We're lucky. They dropped her off, they did that for us."

"*Cowards,*" said Laura.

Wes sat back and the whole line of chairs shifted. Cowards would have left her where she was. Bravery got her here. He knew what kind of kid he'd been, a scattering boy, who would not have stopped to think till half a mile away.

Adrenaline flooded your conscience like an engine you then couldn't start. But Helen hadn't been that kind of kid. She had stayed with the boy in distress, the officers of a month ago had said, and the universe had repaid her.

"I'm sorry," said Kit. "I'm so, so sorry." She was still wearing her rose-patterned nightgown, with a pair of silver sandals. She looked like a mythical sleep-related figure: Narcolepta, Somnefaria. As soon as he thought that, Wes felt the need to sleep fall over his head like a tossed sheet.

"Who are they?" Laura suddenly asked Kit. "You must have met them."

"She'd leave me somewhere and make me promise not to budge."

"French boys?"

"I don't know!" said Kit.

Every night for a week, Helen had snuck out to see some boys. She had met them on one of the sisters' walks together; the next walk, she sat Kit down on a park bench with a book and told her to stay put. At night, she took either her mother or her father's American cell phone; Kit slept with their shared phone set to vibrate under her pillow. When Helen wanted to be let back in, she called till the buzzing phone woke up Kit, who snuck down the stairs to open the front door.

Kit was going to be the wild child. That's what they had said, back when she was a two-year-old batting her eyes at waiters, giggling when strangers paid attention. It was going to be Kit sneaking out of the house in the middle of the night, Helen lying to protect her.

You worked to get your kids to like each other and this was what happened.

They went to the ICU. When Kit saw her sister, she began to cry again. "I don't know anything else," she said, though nobody was asking. "I just—I don't know."

Laura stayed by the door. She put her arm around Kit. She could not look at anyone. Wes thought she was about to pull the wheeled screens around her, as though in this country that was how you attended your damaged child. A mother's rage was too incandescent to blaze unshaded. "How do they even know she fell?" she whispered. "Maybe she was hit with something, maybe—was she raped?"

Wes shook his head uneasily. There was Helen in the bed. They needed to go to her.

"How do you *know*?" said Laura.

"They checked."

"I will kill them," she said. "I will track down those boys. I hate this city. I want to go home." At last she looked at Wes.

"We can't move her yet."

"I know," said Laura, and then, more quietly, "I want to go home *now*."

Well, after all: he'd had the width of three *arrondissements* to walk, getting ready to see Helen. As a child he'd been fascinated by the bends—what scuba divers got when they came to the surface of the ocean too fast to acclimate their lungs to ordinary pressure. You had to be taken from place to place with care. Laura had gone from apartment to taxi-cab to hospital too quickly. Of course she couldn't breathe.

But it didn't get any easier as the day went on. She looked at Helen, yes, and arranged her hair with the pink rattail comb a nurse had left behind. All the while, she delivered a muttering speech, woven of curses: she cursed their decision to come to Paris; she cursed the midmorning's comically elegant doctor who inflated her cheeks and puffed when asked about Helen's prognosis; she damned to hell the missing boys.

"They *say* boys," said Laura, "but if they didn't see them, how do they know?"

"We need to solve the problems we can, honey," said Wes.

That afternoon Kit and Laura took the Métro back to the city. Kit was seven, after all.

He didn't get to the apartment until ten. Laura was already in bed but awake. They talked logistics. In two days they were scheduled to fly home. It made more sense for Laura to stay with Helen—she was a freelancer, Wes's classes started in a week—but there was the question of language. The question of Paris.

"I'll stay," Wes said. They were in bed. Beyond, M. Petit's apartment was silent. Kit was asleep in the twin bedroom on the other side of the hall.

Laura nodded. "Shouldn't we all?" Then she answered herself. "Third grade."

"Third grade," said Wes. School started for Kit in a week, too. She shouldn't miss it. "We've got the phones. Imagine what this used to be like." They'd talked about that, how appallingly easy technology made it to be an expat these days. "Listen, I'm sure, I'm sure in a week, or two—we can bring her home."

Neither of them could wonder aloud what change in Helen's condition would allow that.

"Where will you stay?" Laura asked.

"Oh, God. I hadn't thought."

He knocked the next morning on M. Petit's door. Two young men answered. One of them was holding some dark artwork in a large frame. The other was folding a cup into one of the panes of an unfurled newspaper.

"*Bonjour,*" said Wes, and then he couldn't think of what to say.

"English?" said one of the men, a balding redhead.

"Yes. American." Wes pointed at the door behind him.

"Ah!" said the redhead, and Wes could see M. Petit in his expression. In both of their faces, actually. His sons. The redheaded man explained: their father had died suddenly, unexpectedly.

"Oh, no," said Wes. "I am sorry." He felt a tender culpability, as though his own disaster had seeped through the walls and killed the old man. He tried to remember the last time he'd heard M. Petit's morning routine.

"So you see," said the redhead. "We must pack."

"We've had an accident," said Wes. "My family. An emergency. I was wondering if I could extend the lease."

"Ah, no. No. Actually my daughter is moving in, next week, with her husband. Newlyweds."

Wes nodded. He felt a tweak in his chest, disappointment or despair. He needed to stay, as cheaply as possible, and he couldn't imagine where he might start looking for shelter, or how long it would take.

"But," said the son. "Would you like—you could perhaps rent this?" He pointed at the floor of M. Petit's apartment, the same warm burnt orange tiles as next door. Wes peered down the hallway into the murk. "Very sudden, you see."

"Yes," Wes said. "Thank you. Merci. Merci mille fois."

He took the semester off from school. His department head said they'd figure things out so he could still draw a salary—a course reduction, a heavier load in the spring. Better to solve it now for everyone involved than to wonder every day whether Wes might be coming back.

On the day of the flight he and Laura and Kit went to the hospital. Kit said goodbye to her sister tearfully, lovingly, crawled into the bed and stroked Helen's hair and said, "I promise, I promise, I promise." What promise? Wes thought she would tell him when they said goodbye at the airport, though when they got there Kit was awkward, unhappy, her hands bunched under her chin as though, if he tried to draw her close, she would fight him off with her elbows. "Goodbye, Kitty," he said. She nodded.

He thought then that he should find a place to lie down, like Helen. You said goodbye to someone differently if they were supine. But he didn't see any benches, and if he lay on the ground, he'd be pummeled by European feet and suitcases. Security, perhaps. Send ahead his belt and shoes (only in prisons and airports did a stranger tell you to take them off). Put his sad sorry body down. Kit might not fall for it at first. *"Dad,"* she would say, humiliated, because now she had to bear the humiliation for her sister as well. But then, surely, as he disappeared, his head, shoulders, beltless waist, as the agents saw the truth of his kidneys, his empty pockets, she would run to him, grab at his feet—no. Feet first, so that she had enough time to whisper that promise in his ear.

In the end he picked her up. He couldn't remember the last time he'd done that. Her toes knocked against his shins. "We'll talk every day," he said.

"I know," she answered.

Then he kissed Laura. "Call me when you get in."

"It'll be too late."

"No," he said. "Not possible."

He watched them go through the checkpoint. Laura kept waving, *go, go,* but he couldn't, not until they disappeared from sight.

He took the train back into the city, to move his suitcase into M. Petit's apartment. The furniture was ancient, fringed, balding. The windows looked onto the courtyard, not the street. It felt like the depressed cousin of the apartment where they'd been so happy. The right place to be, in other words. The bathroom had a slipper tub, deep and short, with a step to sit on. How had M. Petit climbed into it? The bed was in a loft. No octogenarian should have to use a ladder to go to sleep. Everything in the world now looked like something to fall from. He decided he would sleep on the little L-shaped couch, in case M. Petit had died in the bed. He put the sea-serpent lampshade in the middle of the coffee table and fell asleep. He surprised himself by sleeping through the night. He checked the phone: a text from Laura, *Arrived will call in my morning/your afternoon*. He went, for the third day, to the hospital.

The border between consciousness and coma was not as defined as Wes had been taught by television to expect. They'd stopped sedating her. Helen did not come bursting to the surface, as though from a lake. She rose out of unconsciousness by millimeters over the next few days. Her nose woke up. Her forehead. Her cheeks. Her eyes. The pressure in her skull abated; the ventric tube came out.

She had the daft look of a saint. Even her hands were knotted together at her chest, as though in prayer. Her mouth was open. The nurses combed her hair, what was left of it, and then called in the hospital's hairdresser, who cropped it like Jeanne d'Arc's.

In the hospital Wes studied Helen as he had when she was an infant. Around and around her face, the knotted fingers, the angles of her shoulders. She wasn't a baby, of course. She was a girl, thirteen in a month, with breasts, whose body would keep going further into adulthood no matter whether her brain could catch up. The doctors said it was still too early to tell.

He tried to find his daughter in this girl's expression, but she'd been so completely revised, and then he tried to comfort himself: Helen was past worry. The worst would not happen to her because it already had. There were no decisions to be made right now. She wouldn't die. She was, for the moment, beyond any psychological complexities. He had to be here. That he could manage.

At the end of every day, he walked back to Paris, all four

and a half miles: beneath the Périphérique, through the seventeenth arrondissement, down le boulevard Malesherbes, and he spoke to Laura, his ear throbbing against the plastic of the phone. She sounded far away, relieved. He related the latest diagnosis: they were still assessing whether Helen's brain injury was focal or diffuse. Her brain was still swollen in her skull. It might take her years to recover. Laura told him the news of America: the insurance company was being extraordinarily good at working with the hospital; the cell-phone company would not forgive the nearly thousand-dollar bill for Helen's purloined Parisian phone calls and text messages. Sometimes Kit was there, though there were swimming lessons and playdates and flute lessons or just the sound of the slamming door as she went outside.

"We miss you," Laura would say.

"We miss you, too," he answered.

"*You* miss us. Helen doesn't miss anything."

"We don't know."

"I feel it."

"OK," he said, because she might have been right.

By the time they'd talked themselves out he was back in the third arrondissement, and then he would zag towards the river. He walked as they had their first jet-lagged day, to exhaust himself before climbing the stairs to M. Petit's apartment, so he could fall asleep without hearing the noises of the granddaughter and her husband in that three-quarter bed on the other side of the wall. Or on the sofa, or any corner of his old home. Sometimes he thought, *That's us still, and I am M. Petit,* and he tried to find the part of the wall that bordered on what had been the girls' bedroom. Maybe he would hear them scheme. Maybe this time he could stop it.

Or maybe he'd just hear the neighbors fucking.

One night on the way home he found a little store that catered to Americans, big boxes of sugary cereal, candy bars, and he wanted to buy them for Helen, whose nasogastric tube had just been taken out, though she was fed only purees. The store carried every strain of American crap. French's mustard, Skippy peanut butter, Stove Top stuffing, even Cheez Whiz. He'd been gone long enough from the U.S. that he felt sentimental about the food, and he'd been in Paris long enough to feel superior to it.

Then he saw the red-topped jar of Marshmallow Fluff.

"Something sweet for you," he said to Helen the next morning. He hunted around for a spoon and found only a tongue depressor. That would do.

Helen closed her eyes as the Fluff went in, as her round mouth irised in around the stick. Wes felt electrified. Before this moment Helen had been a blank, as mysterious to him as she must have been to the emergency room when she'd first arrived: a girl who'd dropped from the sky. Unidentified. Cut off from her history.

Now she opened her eyes, and he could see, for the first time, Helen looking out of them, though (he thought) she couldn't see anything. She was sunk in the bottom of a well. Everything above her was hidden in shadows. He could see her trying to make something out. Her mouth, agape, opened further, with muscle, intent, greed: *more*.

He dug out a larger dollop. Closed eyes, closed mouth, but when the tongue depressor went in Helen began to cough. It was a terrible wet sound.

"Are you all right?" he said. He wondered whether he should put his finger in her mouth, scoop it out, and then he did, and Helen bit down. First just pressure, the peaks of her molars, then pain. He tried to pull out his finger. "Wow. Helen," he said. "Helen, please, Helen, help! Help!" and then her jaw relaxed, and he stood with his wet, indented finger, panting.

The doctor on the floor was Dr. Delarche, the tall woman who'd so infuriated Laura. By the time she peered in Helen's mouth all the Fluff had melted away except a wisp on her upper lip.

"What is this?" she asked Helen. She touched her chin, looking over her face. "*Hein?* This sticky thing."

Wes still held his sore finger. "Fluff."

"Floff?" The doctor turned to him. "What is this floff?"

The lidless jar had fallen to the bed—he pulled it out from under the blanket, and inclined the mouth towards the doctor. "Marshmallow, um, *crème,*" he said, pronouncing it the French way. "You put it on bread, with peanut butter."

Dr. Delarche looked incredulous. "No," she said. "This is not good for the body. Even without traumatic brain injury but certainly with. No more floff."

"OK," he said, exhilarated.

His mistake had been to believe that the girl in the bed wanted nothing. But that *was* Helen, and Helen was built of want. She longed, she burned, even if she couldn't move or swallow Marshmallow Fluff. He wished he could find her boys so they could sit on the edge of the bed and read to her; he wished he could take her into the city, let her drink wine.

Well, then. He needed to find what she wanted, and bring it to her.

That evening, after the walk, he found himself on a street that seemed lined with art supplies: a pen shop, a painting shop, a paper store. In the paint shop he bought a pad that you could prop up like an easel, and watercolors in a little metal case with a loop on the back for your thumb, for when you painted *plein air*. It was the sort of thing he'd have bought for the girls in an ordinary time. He hadn't painted himself since graduate school—he'd been a print-maker, and that's what he taught—and it had been even longer since he'd used watercolors. But Helen had. She'd taken lessons at home. Perhaps she could teach him. That's what he would tell her.

"Ah!" said the doctor, when she saw him set up the pad. "Yes. Therapy. Very good. This will help."

They began to paint.

Yes, Helen was there, she was in there. She could not form words. She smiled more widely when people spoke to her but it didn't seem to matter what they said. But with the brush in her hand—Wes just steadying—she painted. At

first the paintings were abstracts, fields of yellow and orange and watery pink (she never went near blue) overlaid
with circles and squares. She knew, as he did not, how to
thin the paint with water to get the color she wanted.

Soon she was moved to a private room on another floor.
The hospital manicurist ("How very Parisian!" said Laura,
when he told her) gave her vamp red toes and fingernails.
Wes's favorite nurse, a small man who reminded him of a
champion wrestler from his high school, devised a brace
from a splint and a crepe bandage to help with the painting,
so that Helen could hold her wrist out for longer, though
she still needed help from the shoulder.

"She's painting," said Wes on the phone. He'd blurted it
out at the end of a conversation, standing in front of the
front door of the building: until then he hadn't realized
he'd been keeping it a secret.

"What do you mean?" asked Laura.

He explained it to her: the brace, the watercolors.

"What is she painting?"

"Abstracts. I'll take a picture, you can see."

There was a silence.

"What?"

"Nothing. I sighed. You mean she's painting like an elephant paints."

"What do you mean?"

"There's an elephant who paints. Maybe more than one.
They stick a brush in its trunk and give it a canvas. The re-
sults are better than you'd think. But it's not really painting,
is it? It's moving with paint. She doesn't know what she's
doing."

"She does," said Wes. "She's getting better."

"By millimeters."

"Yes! Forward."

"What good is forward, if it's by millimeters?" said Laura. "How far can she possibly go?"

"We don't know!"

"I wish she had——" Laura began. "I just don't know what her life is going to be like." Another silence.

Wes knew it wasn't sighing this time. He said, "Listen. I gotta go."

He had not had a drink since the early morning call from the hospital; he'd had the horrible thought he might have woken up and caught Helen sneaking out that night, had he been entirely sober. Now he thought about picking up a bottle of wine to take to M. Petit's. He passed by the gym he'd seen before, which was still open though it was ten at night. A woman sat at street level in a glass box, ready to sign him up. She wore ordinary street clothes, not exercise togs.

"*Bonjour, madame,*" he said. "*Je parle français très mal.*"

"*Ah, non!*" said the woman. "*Très bien.*"

She seemed to be condescending to him, but in a cheerful, nearly American way.

The actual gym was in the basement. By American standards it was small, primitive, but there were free weights—he'd lifted pretty seriously in college—and a couple of treadmills. From then on he came here after his long walk, his phone conversation with Laura, because only exertion blunted the knowledge that Laura wished that Helen had died. He hoped Laura had something to do, to blunt her own knowledge that he knew she felt this way and disagreed.

For some reason one of the personal trainers took a dislike to him, and was always bawling him out in French, for bringing a duffel bag onto the gym floor, for letting his knees travel over his toes when he squatted, for getting in the way of the French people who seemed always to be swinging around broom handles as a form of exercise. The trainer's name was Didier, according to the fliers by the front desk; his hair was shaved around the base of his skull, long on top. Like an *oignon,* Wes thought. Didier drank ostentatiously from a big Nalgene bottle filled with a pale yellow liquid, and it pleased Wes to pretend the guy was consuming his own urine. It was good to hate someone, to have a new relationship of any kind with no medical undertones.

When I've been here a year, he thought one night, as he performed deadlifts in the power rack, *when we find the right place to live, me and Helen—then I'll get a girlfriend.* The thought seemed to have flown into his head like a bird—impossible, out-of-place, smashing around. It didn't belong there. It couldn't get out.

After three weeks, Helen was not just better, but measurably better: she held her head up, she turned to whoever was speaking, she squeezed hands when people said her name.

And she painted. The abstracts had hardened, angled, until Wes could see what she meant. She was painting Paris.

Back in the U.S. they had thought Helen had talent and they'd seized on it, bought her supplies, sent her to classes, not just painting but sculpture, pastel, photography. The problem was content, no better than any suburban American girl's: Floating princesses. Pretty ladies. Ball gowns.

Now she painted stained glass and broken buildings in sunshine, monuments, gardens. He could feel her hand struggling to get things right. She drew faces with strange curves and bent smiles. The first time she signed her name in the corner in fat bright letters Wes burst into tears.

Staff and visitors took her paintings away, without asking, and Wes had to hide the ones he particularly wanted. He was waiting for the right one to mail to Laura, he told himself, but every day's paintings were better than the last. He wanted to send the best one.

One morning he ran into Dr. Delarche on his way to Helen. *"Monsieur,"* she said, and beckoned him. Wes was alarmed. There was never any news from doctors about Helen. He either had to ask or see for himself. And besides, Dr. Delarche worked in the ICU.

"I must ask you something," she said.

He nodded.

"My husband is a documentarist. I wonder—I told him about Helen and her painting. He wishes to do a little film."

"Oh!" said Wes. "Yes!"

The *documentariste* was a shaggy handsome Algerian named Walid who made Wes like Dr. Delarche better: he had an air of joy and incaution. "You don't mind?" he said. His camera was one of those cheap handheld things, a

Flip—Laura's mother had given them one the year before. Wes had better video capabilities on his Nikon, back at the flat. He imagined most of the footage would feature the profile of Walid's wide calloused thumb.

He didn't tell Laura about the filming. She would tell him to throw the doctor's husband out of the room. *Do not turn our child into a freak show,* she would have said—

—but Wes knew that was all that Helen had ever really wanted.

Not love, and not quotidian attention: since she was a child she liked to scare and alarm her parents and strangers and he did not believe anymore that it was some sort of coded message—a cry for love! She just wants you to talk to her! Helen wanted love but no ordinary sort. She wanted people to gape. Left alone in the U.S., she would have not just had her nose pierced, nor her ears, she would have got not just black forked tattoos across the small of her back: she would have obliterated herself with metal and ink, put plugs in her earlobes, in her lips. People would have stared at her. They would have winced and looked away. She wanted both.

Now she had both.

He was not stupid enough, not optimistic enough, to think that she would have made this bargain herself. She wouldn't have given up the boys in some strange part of Paris, offering her wine, watching her do something stupid before she fell. But if she were in bed in a hospital, she would—not *would,* but *did*—want to be the most interesting girl in the bed who ever was. Filmed and fussed over.

Called, by the more dramatic of the nurses, miraculous. Visited by the sick children of the hospital, who were brought by well-meaning religious volunteers.

Helen's room was a place of warmth and brightness. Everyone said so. Walid kept filming, though Wes was never clear to what end.

"Perhaps," said Walid one day, "when we are finished, the boys she was with? They will see this film."

"They could come to visit!" said Wes.

"Eh?" said Walid. He stopped filming and regarded Wes. "Turn themselves in. Repent. That's terrible, to abandon a girl, isn't it? You are American and you want them dead," he explained. "We, of course, do not believe in the death penalty. Anymore: we have had our bumps. But still. Terrible."

"She is an inspiration," said Dr. Delarche one day as Wes and Helen painted. "This is not a bad thing." Dr. Delarche leaned against the wall in the lab coat she made look chic: it was the way she tucked her hands in the pockets. Since Wes had agreed to let Walid film, she came to the room nearly every day, though never when Walid himself was around. Maybe she had a crush on him, though that seemed very un-French. He had a crush on her.

"The light in the paintings," she said to him. "Like Monet, *hein*?"

"God, no," said Wes. "I hate Monet. Where you going, Helen? Red? Here's red."

"Renoir," suggested Dr. Delarche.

"Worse. No," said Wes, "I will take your side against the Italians with wine, and coffee, and even ice cream, but painting? They have you beat. The French are too pretty."

"We are pretty," Dr. Delarche agreed. "And cheese also, we are better. Wine, of course. Everyone know that. So then. You are making plans?"

He shook his head pleasantly, not knowing what she meant.

"Soon Helen will go," she said.

"Die?" He stopped his hand and felt the pressure of Helen wanting to move, but he pulled the brush from the brace and set it down. He was sorry he'd said the word in front of her.

"Ah, no!" said Dr. Delarche. She sounded insulted that he'd misunderstood her so badly. The French, in his experience, were often insulted by other people's stupidity. "From here."

"To another hospital."

"Home. To the United States. You will talk to the social workers, see what they know—she is better. Of course. She is much, much better, and now she is strong enough to travel. So, hurrah, isn't it? You will go home to your family."

"Of course," he said.

He left the hospital then; he almost never walked out of the building during the day. Neuilly-sur-Seine looked like a stage set built by someone who had never been to Paris and imagined it was boring: clean nineteenth-century buildings with mansard roofs, little cafés that served coffee in white china cups, nothing notable or seedy. He thought about taking Helen back to M. Petit's apartment and he realized that was the real reason he'd started going to the gym: he lifted weights so he could lift Helen. Five flights up. Into the slipper bath. Around Paris, even. He'd walked enough of the city to know it was a terrible place for a wheelchair. No Americans with Disabilities Act, no cutouts in curbs. It would be easier on foot.

He would carry her to the Jardin des Plantes. They would paint the animals in the zoo, visit the mosaicked tearoom at the mosque. In his head he saw her improve by time lapse: her mouth closed, she sat straighter. He didn't care that their short-term visas would expire in two weeks. He could not picture them in America.

If she could not walk or speak in America, then she would not walk or speak for the rest of her life, and that was something he would not accept.

But when he called Laura on his way home that night, she said she was coming in two days. Kit would stay with friends. Her brother had given her a last-minute ticket. She wanted to see for herself how Helen was doing.

As Wes waited at the airport he worried he wouldn't recognize his wife—he always worried this, when meeting someone—and his heart clattered every time the electric double doors opened to reveal another exhausted traveler. When she came out, of course, he knew her immediately, and he felt the old percolation of his blood of their early dates, when he loved her and didn't know what would happen. *That's her,* he thought. She crossed the tile of the airport and it was no mirage of distance. She fell into him and he loved her. He felt ashamed of every awful thought he'd had about her for the past weeks. They held each other's tiredness awhile.

"You feel different," she said. "Thinner. You look kind of wonderful. How's Didier?"

"I hate him with every fiber of my being. You look more than kind of wonderful."

She shook her head. Then she said, "I don't want to go back there."

"Where?" he said. "Oh. Well, that's where Helen is."

"That's not where Helen is."

"She's better. She's—she'll know you're there." As soon as he'd said it he realized he'd been telling Laura the opposite, to comfort her: Helen didn't really know who was there and who wasn't and therefore it was all right that Laura and Kit were thousands of miles away in America.

"Really?" said Laura.

"Yes."

"How does she show it?"

They headed down to the airport train station. Wes had already bought the tickets back into Paris. At last he said, "She's painting. She's still painting, Laura."

The train stopped in front of them with a refrigerated hiss and they stepped on. "I know."

"What?"

"Kit showed me. On YouTube. I mean, it doesn't show her painting. She's not really, is she. I don't believe it."

He had heard about news traveling on the Internet, but he imagined that was gossip, or affairs, or boss badmouthing: it traveled locally, not from country to country.

"Who's really painting?" said Laura. "The therapist, or someone. One of those religious women. In some of the shots you can see a hand steadying her elbow."

"Helen," said Wes. "I promise. Come on. She'll show you."

At the Gare du Nord, Laura said, "Let's take a cab. Let's go see Helen."

"Don't you want to drop off your suitcase?"

She shook her head. "I wish you'd found another place to stay."

They went to the stand along the side of the station. He hadn't been inside a taxi since their first day in Paris. Mornings, he went to the hospital underground, afternoons he came back by foot. He felt suddenly that every national weakness a people had was evident on its highways.

"Do you have cash?" Laura asked as they pulled up.

"I thought you did."

"I just got here. I have dollars."

He dug through his pockets and found just enough. They stepped outside.

"I hate it here," Laura said, looking at the clean façade of the hospital.

"I know. I hate it, too."

"No. You're better than me. You don't hate it. You hate the situation. That's the right response. Me, I want to run out the door and never come back. I would, if I could."

"This way," he said. "They moved her."

At first Wes was struck by how good Helen looked, the pink in her cheeks, the nearly chic haircut. Then he glanced at Laura and then he understood how little, really, their daughter had changed. It had been six weeks. She looked dazed and cheerful. She couldn't speak.

"Hi, honey," said Wes. "Look. Mommy's here."

"Oh, God," said Laura.

"Sshh," said Wes.

But Laura was by the bed. She touched Helen's cheek. "Honey," she said. "Sweetheart. Shit." She looked down the length of Helen and pulled up the sheet: her bent knees with the pillow between, the wasting muscles, the catheter tube. She shook her head, rearranged the sheet. "I know, I know what you think of me, Wes."

"I don't—"

"It's not that it's not her. It's that—whoever this person in the bed is, she's where my Helen should be. That's what I can't get over and it's what I know I have to."

Laura was wearing a dress she had bought in the July sales when they'd first arrived, red, with blue embroidered flowers on the shoulders like epaulets. She had belted it too tight. She had lost weight, too.

"Just sit," he said to her. "There are chairs. Here's one. We'll paint. Shall we paint, Helen?"

He wound the brace around her wrist, always a pleasing task, and slid in Helen's favorite long-handled brush, meant for oils, not watercolors. He propped up the pad on the wheeled table that came over the bed, got the water, the colors, dampened the paints. They began.

"You're doing it," said Laura.

"No," he said patiently. "I'm just steadying her hand."

"Then let go," said Laura.

He did, and he believed it would happen: her hand

would sail up, like a bird tossed in the air. It would just keep flying. Yes, that was right. If anything, he wanted to tell Laura, he was holding her hand too still, he was interfering. She didn't need him anymore.

But her hand went ticking down to the bottom of the page, and stopped.

Helen's jaw worked, and Laura and Wes watched it. She had not made a noise in weeks. She did not make one now. The short haircut looked alternately gamine and like a punishment. Wes picked her hand back up, placed it, let go. Tick, tick, to the bottom of the page.

"So you see," said Laura.

Wes shook his head. No. She'd needed the help but he was not capable of those paintings.

And if he was, what did that mean? The paintings were what was left of Helen.

"She's not a fraud," said Wes.

"No, I don't think she is," said Laura. "I don't think she's anything. She's not at home, Wes."

"Isn't she?" said Wes.

"No," said Laura. She tapped her head. "I mean here, in her brain, she's not at home. It doesn't matter where her body is. Her body will be at home anywhere. But it matters where *your* body is. We need to take her home and you, too."

"It isn't just me who's seen it," said Wes.

"Who doesn't love a miracle girl," said Laura, but with love. "I wanted one, too, honestly. I would have loved it, if it had been real."

But, thought Helen—because Helen *was* at home, Helen

heard everything—wasn't it more of a miracle this way? Her mother was right. She could not move her hands: that was her father. But she saw the pictures in her head, those fields with the apartment blocks, that golden light—and she couldn't move her hand to get them on the paper. Her father did. There was the miracle everyone spoke about, in English and in French. The visiting nuns said it was God, but it was her father who took her hand and painted the pictures in her head. Every time he got them right: the buildings, the light posts, those translucent floating things across her field of vision when she wasn't exactly looking at anything, what as a child she thought of as her conscience—*floaters,* her father once told her they were called. "I have them, too," he'd said. They were worse in the hospital, permanent static. She saw, he painted the inside of her snowglobe skull, all those things whizzing around when she fell—the water tower on top of the building, the boy who'd kissed her, the other boy who'd pushed her, those were their faces in the corner of the page, the bottles of wine she'd drunk—back home she'd had beer and peppermint schnapps and had drunk cough syrup, but not wine. Wine was everything here. Those boys would come visit her. They'd promised they would when they dropped her off. She had to stay put. *Don't let her take me, Daddy.* Her mother hadn't looked her in the eye since she'd come into the room, but when had she, ever, ever, ever, thought Helen. All her life, she'd been too bright a light.

"Careless Helen," said Laura, and then to Wes, "Do you know, I think I've only just forgiven her."

"What for?" asked Wes.

She rubbed her nose absentmindedly. "Funny smell. What is that?"

Not medicine nor illness: the iridescent polish the manicurist had applied to Helen's toes.

In order to wake up every morning, thought Wes, he'd convinced himself of a lot of things that weren't true. He could feel some of his beliefs crumble like old plaster—life in Paris, walking the streets with Helen in his arms, revenge on Didier, even Dr. Delarche's crush. Of course they would go back to the States, where Kit was, they would talk to experts, they would find a facility, they would bring Helen home as soon as they could, where she would be visited by Addie of the braces and the clarinet, and boys from her school. She might never walk again. But her body would persist. It was broken but not failing. She was theirs for the rest of their lives, and then Kit would inherit her. That was what Laura had seen from the first day, and it had crushed her, and she was only just now shifting that weight from her chest.

Helen painted. That was real. He knew his own brain, what it could make up and what it couldn't. He looked at his wife, whom he loved, whom he looked forward to convincing, and felt as though he were diving headfirst into happiness. It was a circus act, a perilous one. Happiness was a narrow tank. You had to make sure you cleared the lip.

ACKNOWLEDGMENTS

Enormous thanks to Henry Dunow, Susan Kamil, Noah Eaker, Ann Patchett, Duchess Goldblatt, Paul Lisicky; to the American Academy in Berlin, the Radcliffe Institute for Advanced Study, and the Bogliasco Fellowship Program for miraculous support; to the editors who have published these stories in magazines and anthologies, including John Freeman, Robin Black, Adrienne Miller, Joyce Carol Oates, Geraldine Brooks, Allison Wright, W. Ralph Eubanks, and particularly Michael Ray of *Zoetrope: All-Story,* who got me writing short stories again with the right question at the right time.